Dead Kelly

Special thanks to my brother Steve Norris for the Cover art.

Consider the moment just before you die…

 A fleeting glimpse at your entire life's story within a microsecond of time. Like a lightning bolt flashing your journey through life, before passing onto that great departure lounge in the sky. A catalogue of all the little things you had done or perhaps, things you wished you had done before your expiry date ran out. Was it is just a myth that your story played out like a fast forwarding movie in which you see every grand event whizzing past, or indeed a real phenomenon with that camera flash of life prior to the proverbial bucket being kicked… But then who would know?
Only those about to shake off their mortal coil would truly have an inkling of that final leap into the great beyond.
And maybe it is exactly what happened to Clarence Bunn moments before he heard the sound of his own body hitting the ground at high speed… Thud!!

Nothing to see here
The sun rose over the ocean, shining beams of light through the post storm clouds and onto the figure of a man standing on the sea wall; a clay pipe poking out from his scruffy, twig filled beard. Quite a strange sight to behold he was too, with a sea gull balancing upon every available surface of him as he scanned the shore for debris.

 "Shush ya pesky birds…" he muttered, while shielding his eyes from the morning sun as it reflected off of the sea like a billion brilliant stars twinkling upon the oceans gentle tide. "Somethin' be out there" he said to no one in particular as the birds flapped and pooped about him, screeching and trying to get at the fish heads that lined the pockets of his filthy wax rain coat.

 He was known as the Gull man, through never being without a large white bird on or about him at any one time and the white streaks of dried poop over his wax clad shoulders told a tale of his unkempt devotion to his feathered friends. He had been around for so many years that no one really took a great deal of notice of him anymore, he just blended into the background, relatively unnoticeable to the world around him like the birds he resided with. Although a menace and sometimes just a shadow of disregard to some, he was as much a part of the little town of Hybrook and its quirky ways as the church with its skull filled crypt or the bakers that had seen more than its fair share of fires. The Gull man was just, well, there. Some of the older folk of Hybrook had known the young Gull man but his real name had sadly disappeared long ago, taking with it his identity, self respect and his sanity.

But his life hadn't always been that way, it had begun happily and humbly in a small hut by the sea. Born to a fisherman and his wife and raised to have a love for all things nautical, his father had pushed the boy to love the ocean and all of her ways as he had done. But it had been the avian population that had gripped the lads heart and imagination and as he grew, so too did his kinship with the great, white herring gull. He would often stare for hours, watching the birds as they floated in the sky, sketching with charcoal onto yellowed paper as the gulls and terns danced on the slipstreams of wind; their white feathers glowing like ghosts against the grey overcast skies above and beyond the ocean. He would often wish to be up there, flying high in the air with not a care in the world but which direction the breeze would take him. A free spirit of the sky, wisping between pockets of wind and hovering like a ghostly winged cloud. His life had been simple, perfect and care free in that small hut by the sea until one stormy night when he had been awoken by the sound of his mother's screams and muffled voices of men. He learned that night that his father had been lost at sea, taken by the unforgiving ocean that he had once loved so dearly and into the cold, relentless arms of the deep, never to be seen again. And from that very moment, his life would be doomed to change, the peace, perfection and warmth; the days of laughter and celebration gone and never to return like a rock being tossed far into the dark salty depths. And then the nightmares began, flashes of white feathers flecked with blood beneath storm clouds that travelled at high speed across a bright, luminescent sky and below, the blackness, the endless blackness of the sea, deep and swirling with whirlpools of frozen darkness that seemed to beckon for death. Reaching out through a deep green haze of water he would grasp at visions,

monsters so barely visible through the deep haze of stormy seas, but the seemingly recognisable faces would push through bubbling screams as his father and the other lost faces of his past. He would scream bubbles into nothing but cold, frightful, rolling waves that smashed against rocks with a sound that almost deafened until the silence came, every night it would come and consume the boys dreams and every night he would wake, soaking with sweat and with the smell of the tide still haunting his nostrils with its ghostly scent. If not a year later his mothers mind finally followed her fractured heart and she was taken from the family home to a special place, leaving the boy alone with just his thoughts and only the birds for company!
And that's how his life was to be from then on, just a lone man and the gulls. His mind and soul lost to the winds like sand falling from the opening fists of a lost child splitting and separating into a beach of nothingness!

But now, as the tide slowly retreated and along with its flotsam and jetsam of timber and old broken whiskey barrels it left something unusual, something new and mysterious. The old man clambered down onto the beach and trudged across the pebbles towards the shape by the shoreline, muttering to himself and puffing on him pipe like funny little steam train, "Fortune favours the man who watched and no better time than after a good ol' storm," he muttered.

Sometimes the sea would leave sumptuous treasures of tobacco, ale, whiskey and on the rare occasion the strangest of sea monsters would be washed up on the beach. Once he had even found a dead whale, it had been his treasure and he had made candles and trinkets and things from its body, every part of the creature had been used and nothing left to waste and some parts he had even sold to the towns folk. But this time, as he neared this particular thing, it became apparent that it was not just a mere 'thing' but a body; the body of a girl, laying sodden and face down to the pebbles with limbs spread out like a starfish. A gull stood on the girl's head and pecked some seaweed from her hair as the tidal sea foam pulled at her feet, perhaps trying to reclaim the body as its own with a hope of swallowing it up and sending it to a life of service with ol' Davy Jones. The bird tilted its head and looked at the scruffy man with its beady yellow eyes, "Bub bub bub," it said.

"What ya say bird?"

"Bub Bub," it replied.

"Ya reckon she be dead?" He inspected the body with a large, glassy left eye and puffed on his little clay pipe.

"Bub Bub Bub," said the Gull again.

The Gull man mumbled something incomprehensible as he shooed the bird away, "Do ya be dead there girl?"

The girl said nothing, nor did she move, apart from the glistening sea salt that dried in her deep auburn hair.

"Yar, he were right… Ya be dead girl."

He scratched his beard, something fell from it, and he mumbled some more.

Within the hour a large group of people had gathered around the corpse, some had dogs, others had fishing rods and a small boy poked the dead girl inquisitively with a stick.

"Move along, Move along." A policeman pushed his way through the crowd. "What's all this then, nothing to see hee…Oh!" His words were stopped short as he set his eyes on the corpse. PC Brash had been the local Bobby in Hybrook for years and before him it had been his father who had been sheriff and before that his father's father had been some kind of peace keeper and so on for as far back as the towns records had given the pleasure of remembering. There was, in actual fact, a Brash in most of the towns, cities and villages in the south east of the country and they all wore the police uniform with pride. Some were regular beat Bobby's while others were in the plain clothes divisions as detectives, but they all had the genes, the hefty frame, the red hair and the jolly, beardy face that had been the male, and sometimes female, Brash family look for generations. It is also believed that the Brash family had expanded out from England and across the seas in both directions like a friendly plague of copper topped coppers, all ready to fight crime in the Brash family style, which usually meant a clip around the ear or in the more severe cases, a Billy club across the noggin. This particular PC Brash however, wore a heavy moustache that joined big ginger sideburns which then, in turn usually disappeared up into his helmet; but this time Brash held the helmet in his hands, respectfully for the dead girl. A voice from the crowd called out "Is she a mermaid constable?" As the hubbub of chattering speculation began to catch on another voice piped up, "Maybe she's a sea witch, I've heard they eat your kiddies

when you're not looking."
Lots more mumbling travelled round the group as new ideas were passed around like a bag of sweets.
"Or one of those kipper people from Atlantis," suggested an old lady from the back, trying to give the best and most plausibly ridiculous answer.
Brash crouched next to the cadaver and placed his hand on her head, "Poor thing, don't look like foul play though, but ya never know," he stood up cleared his throat, "Fetch the doctor," called the constable to no one in particular.
 A faint mumbling chorus of 'fetch for the doctor' travelled out through the gathering like a Ripple on water; until the small boy with the stick ran from the group, up to the high street to the doctor's house. A moment later and a young man dashed across the beach, black leather medical bag in hand and the small, stick welding boy in tow followed by a Jack Russell they had picked up along the way that was hopping frantically at his heels like a hairy, four legged pogo stick!
 "What's happened here Brash?" Gasped the doctor, panting and still buttoning up his waistcoat.
 "Poor things dead, well as far as I can make

out anyways."

The doctor crouched down and felt for a pulse in the girls neck, "Hmm!" He placed his stethoscope onto her back to listen for a moment. "Hmm," he said again "Nothing…" there was a dramatic pause before he continued, "I'm afraid you're right constable." He stood and turned to the audience theatrically, looking out wistfully into the distance beyond the crowd of expectant townsfolk, "She's dead!"

There was a dramatic gasp from the onlookers as if the news of the girls obvious demise had been a complete surprise to them all... The doctor turned back round to observe the body for a second look and then, lighting his pipe he eyed constable Brash, "So do you know what happened here?"

"No Doctor, I questioned the first on the scene but he just mumbled something about seaweed and then wandered off."

The young doctor looked at his pocket watch and then frowned at the Bobby, "Do you notice something strange about her Wilf?"

The policeman, helmet still clutched to his chest, shook his head. "Dunno Doctor," said Brash as he scratched at his chin for a moment, "Well she smells a bit like fish but…"

"Look at the skin."

"Looks pretty much like a deadun to me."

"Look closer Wilf… She seems to have been in the water for a good while judging by the wrinkling of her finger tips, but…" A puff of pipe smoke rose between the two men as the doctor mused upon the situation, "… But she hasn't swelled… at all… Nothing! Her lips aren't even blue as would be suggestive of a drowning."

"Well yes, you would've thought she'd at least have been nibbled a bit by the fishes too sir… You know what those little buggers are like, now just yesterday I said…" But the policeman's words were cut short as the Doctor interrupted.

"That's the thing, nothing has even touched her by the looks of it; seems we need to get her to Ashwood as swiftly as possible for further investigation what?"

"What?" Said the Bobby, who had obviously drifted off somewhere about lunchtime. "Oh! Yes, but we 'av good morticians round 'ere Doctor, why Mr. Fratnal of Bakers Barn is a fine gentleman and has quite an eye for this sort of thing if I may say so; he had the pleasure of opening up old Mr Fagg." He plonked his helmet back onto his head and continued as he clipped the strap under his chin. "You remember him, full of maggots when they opened him up, poor old bugger, he was like a sack of wiggling rice he was."

 The doctor raised an eyebrow, "Hmm" he said, "But they have forensically trained experts in the city and mark my words those chaps will find out what or who killed this poor young girl…" The young man looked out to the sea and thoughtfully sucked on his pipe again, "Something is a foot and by Jove I intend to find out what."

Clarence Bunn

A bell pinged as the door pushed open and two identically gaunt gentlemen in top hats and tails entered the waiting room. They were addressed by a burly man standing behind the counter. He was the proprietor of 'Wilkomsir Family Morticians' and by all rights, the finest mortician around, if anyone knew how to cut up a body, weigh the organs and stuff them back in again, it was Angus Wilkomsir. "Ah gentlemen, do come in, you'll find Mrs. Scrubshole has been prepared to our usual exquisite standards." His voice rumbling in a deep but soft Scottish accent. Bowing a little, he led the men through a heavy red curtain and to the back room where a skinny young boy was buffing the bronze plaque of a large oak coffin with the sleeve of his shirt.

Wilkomsir coughed to get the boys attention but his attempt at subtlety had no effect. "Bunn! Shoo!" He called, looking at the young men and raising an impatient eyebrow, "Ach, I must apologise for Clarence, he's my apprentice ya see, he's adopted, bit queer in the head ya know?"

The two suited gentlemen eyed the boy curiously and raised a suspiciously synchronised eyebrow. But it wasn't personal, the Thead brothers eyed everyone in a distrustful manner because as the local undertakers they took their work and to that matter, the entire world about them very, very seriously indeed. They certainly didn't like coming to the morticians at the best of times with its lack of seriousness and disregard for the need to be sombre, and death was indeed a very serious business. Like most of the family trades in the city of Ashwood, Terrence and Tobias Thead had come from a great line of Undertaking Theads. Their father and his twin brother had owned the undertakers before them and so on. Every line had been mysterious and somewhat sinister in every aspect of their lives, as if a bazaar family trait of menacing had been passed down through the generations like a miserable curse of melancholy. Even the Thead women were just as odd and it is said that during child birth the mother of Terence and Tobias remained silent and stern of appearance throughout the whole process of bearing the twins, as if entirely unimpressed by what was occurring. And when the twins were finally born they never cried, they merely stared at the poor young midwife with such utter contempt and disgust that the poor girl fled the room in tears.

 The pale assistant boy shuffled sideways with his head down and his big grey eyes looking up like a scolded puppy. He had always been afraid of the brothers, they never seemed to age and with a name that was an anagram of DEATH, well it just chilled young Clarence to the bone. Even at school they had been a very disturbing pair of individuals and everyone, including the bullies, would steer well clear of the brothers through some ominous sense of doom and foreboding that seemed to follow them like a scary black cloud!

 "Yes Mr. Wilkomsir, sir… Very sorry sir, Mr. Wilkomsir," stuttered the lad, as he sidled off.

 Wilkomsir led the twin gentlemen to the casket and opened its top end to reveal the petrified old lady. Now, to the average observer with no prior knowledge of the old lady, it would be assumed that the mortician had been rather excitable, if not a little overzealous with the makeup, but in actual fact, the late Mrs. Scrubshole had been a great lover of cosmetics and would, on every occasion look as if she had been savagely attacked by an angry trowel full of grease paints. She was one of those old ladies that believed she was still in her 20's and who lived in a constant denial of her true age, which in fact had been a mystery to even her all the way up to her passing. She would often be the one pinching the bottoms of young gentlemen, and needless to say, she had sadly died a spinster.

"Hmm," said Terrence Thead as he observed the corpse with his infuriatingly raised eyebrow of mistrust.

"Umm," suggested Tobias Thead, poking the old woman's face with his bony finger.

The twins turned in a synchronized movement, nodded once and then Terrence reluctantly handed over a large bag of coins to the mortician.

Mr. Wilkomsir squeezed the bag suggestively, said "ooh," with a big red faced beaming at the twins, "Nice doing business with ya gents."

In a back room sat Clarence. He had been at 'Wilkomsir Family Morticians' for almost sixteen years, ever since his father had lost him in a game of poker at the age of three and had then, by some misplaced finger of fate been fostered by the Wilkomsirs. It turned out that Clarence's father had owed a lot of money to a lot of rather undesirable people and had wound up being bludgeoned to death by a hired gentleman in a bowler hat and who had such hideous facial scars that he was forced into a permanently twilight occupation. Unfortunately for Clarence, the first he knew about his fathers demise was when his broken body had come through the Morgue doors to be embalmed and he had had to watch as the policeman explained in rather too much gruesome detail how the man had died. It hadn't been at all nice but Clarence didn't cry, he merely stood listening to the constable, taking in every horribly disturbing word and the pitiful glances of the grownups.

 Now withdrawn, quiet and with an unhealthy obsession with the dead it was no surprise that the boy only had a handful of friends, one being young Bob, the boy who delivered Mr. Wilkomsirs 'Morticians Monthly Muse' newspaper and another being mad Mr. Busby who lived in the bins in the ally out the back. Clarence wasn't entirely sure why Mr Busby lived out in the bins but he had learned some interesting words from him. However, the boy did have two very sincere friends in old Mr. and Mrs. Leech from over the road. They had taken to the boy when he was small and Mr. Leech had discovered the little chap hiding in their nieces Wendy house. It was only the impeccable baking skills of Mrs. Leech that had finally coaxed the boy from the wooden house and from then, they would let him play in their garden, they were like grandparents to young Clarence and the closest thing to a really caring family he had.

Mr. Leech drove a big yellow carriage, pulled by old Nelly and he charged folk for the privilege of a lift. He also dabbled in taxidermy, so it was hardly surprising that Mr. Leech introduced himself as the city's one and only, official taxi driving taxidermist. It had a ring to it and added a little something for his customers to take home with them and for a little extra coin they could also take home a very professionally stuffed sparrow, but for those special customers he had a little box that had a bow on it and within he kept a rather small but elite selection of tits. Mr leech loved those tits, stuffed with the kind of devotion a gourmet chef would give a chicken.

Clarence had tried the stuffing of small animals once or twice, and it was not unlike embalming a human, but it lacked a certain personal touch he thought. He had once explained to Mr. Leech that by replacing the internal organs with straw, it sort of made the animals a little more… well dead. Not like a human, now that was different, they were dead but still had their innards and that, for Clarence, made all the difference and in-fact added a certain amount of life to their death. He had some interesting ideas about life too, and death as it happened. His philosophy was that at the end of ones life, the soul would become like a drop of water where it would be added to the great and eternal ether like a droplet into the ocean. He liked his theory and it pleased him to believe in his own micro-religion for one, although he had never told another soul for fear of being known as a heretic as well as the local weirdo. But weird or not, deep down Clarence believed he would one day be the best Mortician in the city, if not, the world. However, he wasn't about to start running things just yet and as Mr. Wilkomsir told him, if he didn't buck his ideas up, he would never amount to anything. The poor young man had no idea which ideas he needed to buck up and even if he did, he didn't know how an idea even went about such a bucking. He didn't really understand people anyway, well the ones that were alive that is, but the dead, now they were a whole different kettle of fish. He liked the dead, they would never rap his knuckles or throw a shoe brush at him, they would just lay there in a state of deadness and let him carry out his duties in peace. Mr. Wilkomsir had once caught him talking to a corpse and told him that he thought it very strange that a boy of his age would rather have a one sided conversation with a cadaver than with a living person.

"Get ya'self a girlfriend boy," he would shout, but girls weren't interested in pale, skinny morticians assistants who talked about dead things. They only wanted to court soldiers or those brave adventuring gentlemen who flew the airships, but if he was honest, he wasn't really that interested in relationships anyway. He had kissed a girl once though, she had been Mr. Wilkomsirs niece, and well, when he thought about it, she had actually kissed him and he could do nothing about it. It was a lot like a sloppy sink plunger with octopus tentacles he thought as she had lunged at him one Christmas while the entire Wilkomsir family looked on in absolute hilarity, and at one point he had actually feared for his life in the plump, sweaty clutches of Bertha Wilkomsir. Needless to say Clarence was now a little put off by the idea of girls, well for the time being anyway and if they were all like Bertha with their bright frilly dresses and sickly sweet candy shop scent then he was going to remain a bachelor… forever.

He slunk back to his room and slumped down onto the bed. It was a cosy room, just big enough for a small single bed, desk, chest of drawers and a wash basin. Clarence called it home and really didn't mind the size at all as it was the warmest room in the entire building because of it being the engine room for the freezers next door; but that didn't bother him either, knowing that just behind the wall were drawers of corpses. There was another ping followed by footsteps as someone else entered the main foyer upstairs.

"Bunn!" Called Mr. Wilkomsir, causing the lad to jump half out of his skin.
"There's a carriage just arrived round the back. I'm busy out front with young Miss Green, so go help them in will ya boy?"

Clarence huffed as he stood and slipped a pair of goggles over his eyes in case of splashes. It had happened on several occasions to Clarence and he had learned the hard way from it too. There was one occasion where a man had died and then been left in a room in the middle of summer, he had expanded to an enormous size, just like a big purple, man shaped balloon and when Clarence had helped him from the wagon the body had popped, which had taught the boy a valuable lesson on goggle wearing. Maggots and old stinky corpse juice were not the best thing for one's eyes and the incident had left Clarence with a rather nasty infection.

"What now?" He muttered to himself as he padded across the shiny white floor of the 'cutting room' and made his way to the yard. "Another poor old person died in mysterious circumstance I bet." He wondered, tightening the leather apron behind his back and slipping on the big leather gloves that had been handed down to him by someone with substantially larger hands than his own. But as Clarence reached the large sliding doors he was faced by a very large and very grand looking carriage with four black horses before it, very different from the usual carts that arrived with just a bundle of sacking to protect the dignity of the dead within. A very smart young man suddenly appeared from behind the wagon and walked across the yard towards Clarence.

"Good afternoon sir. My name is Doctor Andrew. You must be the Mortician?"

"Well… I'm… Actually the Morticians…" Clarence stuttered, attempting to explain his role.

But the gentleman interrupted, "Jolly good… If you could help me with this and then I shall explain." The doctor opened the back of the carriage and pulled the stretcher half way out. He looked over at Clarence who was still gazing at the large and rather fancy black carriage with his mouth open. "A hand if you would young man."

Clarence jumped from his daydream. He had never seen such a carriage, however something about it made him feel a little uneasy too. The horses with their black plumage on their heads and their eyes that seemed to look panicked, there was just something about them that made Clarence shudder. "Oh… Yes of course." He ran over and grabbed the other end noticing how light the body was.

"Just through here is it?"

"Urm… Yes please," said the boy as he suspiciously glanced back at the scary beasts.

There was a distinct smell of the seaside as they placed the body onto the stainless steel table in the middle of the room.

Clarence grabbed the big black morgue book and opened it to a half filled page. He ran his finger down the list and over the names of its previous occupants. He had always thought how funny it was that every one of us is given a name that you don't get to choose and whether you like it or not, it is yours for your entire life

until you expire and even then it's the identifying thing that makes you memorable to those you leave behind. But in time it is forgotten, by most anyway, except this big black book. It never forgot your name, you were forever in its memories. It was a log of all of those who had passed on and it never ever forgot because it couldn't. There, forever etched in ink on a page within a heavy leather cover we are remembered like a tattoo on the mushed up flesh of a dead tree. The date and the time and the age and even the way in which you shook off your mortal coil, you are there, in someone else's handwriting like a shopping list, all ticked, crossed and dotted. And that was why every entry was added by Clarence, he made sure of it too, to ensure the writing was perfect and respectful to its owner, the way it should be, the final log of ones journey.
"Urm… Name?" He licked the nib of the pen and dipped it into the ink pot.
 "Well unfortunately," said Andrew, pulling back the white sheet. "The poor young thing was found down on the south coast, on the beach and we have absolutely no idea who she was or why she was down there but we can't exclude foul play at this time."
 Clarence peered over at the girls face. She

was very beautiful he thought, in a dead kind of way. He had never seen a girl so pretty in his entire nineteen years and something odd happened in his gut as he looked at her. He carefully and as neatly as he could wrote 'unknown female' into the book and looked at the young Doctor. "How… How did she die?"

The doctor frowned, "Well I imagine she drowned but you are the Mortician right?" He laughed and slapped the boy a little too hard across the shoulder making Clarence stumble a little.

"Well I am actually only the Morticians…" He tried to explain again as he wrote 'suspected drowning' in the book.

"Jolly good," interupted the Doctor again. "Now I've contacted Frances top Forensic scientist, François La Douche and he has said that he will be here by Monday. I assume you can keep her here over the weekend?"

"Urm… Yes…Of…"

"Very well. Now I must be going, but do send an errand boy when Doctor La Douche arrives, I'll be staying at this address, there's a good chap."

And with that, Doctor Andrew slapped a piece of paper into the boys hand and disappeared. Clarence scratched his head and looked at the scrap paper the Doctor had handed him, it was the address of some rather posh apartments in the west end of the city and a far cry from the rough and smokey areas that Clarence was used to. He looked over at the body of the girl again and smiled, screwing up the paper and placing it in this waistcoats breast pocket beneath his leather apron. "Hello," He whispered, "My name is Clarence. Clarence Bunn and I'm here to look after you." He reached over to the tray next to him and picked up a set of tongs, which he then placed either side of the girls head, "I'm just measuring you miss." Clarence then put the tongs against a metal ruler that was secured to the side of the steel table with large rivets and wrote some numbers in another big black mortuary book before continuing to measure the girl. It was a strange ritual to measure the dead thought Clarence because it had absolutely nothing to do with the art of embalming or caring for the dead. It had all been started during one of the many wars fought in one of his Majesty's many colonies against any number of poor, self preserving native tribes by a gentleman called General Burke. He was a top military physician and an avid statistician and he had decided that all dead should be measured for the love of statistics and audits. Clarence frowned at the girl, "You see its all numbers and nonsense, that's all. Just a lot of old cr…"

"Bunn!" The booming voice echoed around the large, white tiled room like a great big angry Scottish bomb going off and Clarence nearly jumped out from his skin, again.

"For the sake of the Gods boy, what have I told you about talking to the corpses? Eh?" He pushed the boy aside and eyed the body. "Now what do we have here?" As Mr. Wilkomsir spoke he pulled on some heavy rubber gloves and popped the goggles over his eyes. "Straight chop 'n weigh is it?"

Clarence grabbed the Scotsman by the wrist. "No sir, Mr. Wilkomsir, actually the man said to wait for a Doctor… Douche bag? I think."

"Doctor La Douche?"

"That was it sir yes."

"Ah for God's sakes. I cannae stand that old sack of frog bones." He moved his pipe around in his mouth, "This must be a murder then if they want him and his gadgets… Bloody scientists." He muttered. "In my day we morticians would do all the work. Chopping here and embalming there and if the corpse had an axe in his heed then ya bloody well knew it were a murder." He muttered and mumbled beneath his breath about the old days and Clarence switched off from the ranting Scotsman Ashe normally found himself doing.

"Well I think it was just suspicious circumstances sir. He said the girl was found on a beach on the south east coast and that the French chap will come on Monday?" Clarence leaned over the girls head again and pushed away her auburn hair from her pale face, before placing his goggles up onto his forehead. "She is very pretty though sir."

Wilkomsir leaned over too and took a draw of his pipe, "Meh…I imagine she was, if you like that kind of thing." And he eyed young Clarence with a very suspicious look indeed. "Right then, let's put her into chiller number eleven I think and pack up for the weekend ey boy?"

"Yes Mr. Wilkomsir sir."

As they slid the body into the cooler, Mr. Wilkomsir placed a large bunch of keys onto the girl's legs. Clarence hated how his boss would do that, these were people and not just an addition to the table top to place things upon.

"Now. You lock up boy. I have family down for the weekend so I won't be around. You'll be ok here on yer own."

As usual it felt like Mr. Wilkomsir was telling Clarence how things should be rather than just asking him outright, but he was used to that; it was the only way of life the boy knew and so he answered with his customary, "Yes sir Mr. Wilkomsir sir." But for the boy the weekend had already been planned like every other weekend and that was why he relished in the fact that Mr Wilkomsir would not be around. Saturday was cleaning day and stoking up on all the essentials for the coming week, and as Mr Wilkomsir would say, "These tools dunne sharpen themselves." And he was right, a sternum wasn't going to be cut with a blunt bone saw and a rusty rib spreader was as much use as trying to open a can of corned beef with a wooden spoon if it hadn't been well lubricated. Everything would be oiled and maintained for Monday, even the make up was set out into its specific places and sometimes tested by the boy, just to experiment of course. But Sunday was the lads favourite day, he would first go round the back, to the bins and ensure that Mr Busby was still alive. The crazy old hobo would normally wake after several minutes and be generally abusive to Clarence, but the boy knew he didn't mean it. And then the best part would come late morning, he

would make sure that the occupants of chillers 1 to 30 were safe and not too lonely, because sadly Clarence knew full well what that felt like. He enjoyed the chats though and every week would normally bring him 30 new people to talk to, each with their own story although Clarence would sometimes have to fill in the blanks, but he knew that if they were looking down, or up, or even sideways from wherever or whatever afterlife they were in, then they would understand and appreciate his kindness.
He looked at the big Scotsman and smiled.
"Have a lovely weekend Mr Wilkomsir sir."
 Angus wrinkled his nose. "I'll need some whiskey to get me ready for the arrival of that old French git!"

Inside number 11

It had just gone midnight and Clarence was still wide awake. He was thinking about the girl in the freezer and wondering what her story was. Maybe she had been thrown from a ship by pirates or had been running from pirates, perhaps she was a pirate. Maybe she was swept from her lovers arms by a wave, or maybe he had pushed her in, but he secretly hoped that no one had done such a ghastly thing because she seemed nice. There were a million and one potential possibilities and as Clarence ran through some of them he stared at the damp spot on the ceiling and imagined. All of a sudden a scrapping sound and a thud broke his thoughts and he sat bolt upright, eyes wide like a possum in the darkness as he listened intently for another sound. He thought for a moment and then a most horrific suggestion popped up in his mind: body snatchers. Mr. Wilkomsir had told him all about body snatchers and had said that they sometimes broke into morgues in the dead of night, and emphasised that it was mostly at weekends, to steal jewellery and gold teeth from the dead, and sometimes they even stole a whole body, so that they could sell them to

the universities or even bones of the dead to make them into potions for potency. Clarence was not entirely sure what type of potency the old man had been referring too, but Angus had clenched his fist and made an upward thrusting gesture with his arm at the same time suggesting it to mean something rather rude.
 Another clatter echoed from next door that sent a chill up his spine and now Clarence hoped that the stories of body snatchers were just a myth or even one of Mr. Wilkomsir's cruel jokes. He did have a way with his evil humour, like hiding in the freezers and pretending to be a zombie, or there was, on more than one occasion that he had used chloroform on the boy and put him inside a freezer, all night. The old Scotsman had found it very amusing but at the time the 8 year old Clarence had not quite seen the funny side of it. But with all the talk at the moment of the burglaries happening in the city too, with rare artefacts being stolen, the lad did not know what to think. Perhaps burglars were in the building to steal everything, although on second thoughts, there was not a great deal in the morgue worth stealing unless the robber enjoyed medical tools and embalming fluids; and that sent another thought flying into Clarence's head like a nine iron

hitting home a golf ball brained idea. Sometimes drunkards would consume embalming fluids among other things due to its intoxicating properties, what if there was a hobo out there? What if his brain had been pickled by years of drinking? What if there was more than one? Clarence had been in the mortician business for several years now and was privy to some rather morbid sights, which included, among others, the opening of the skull to reveal the brain. It was one of his jobs to weigh the organs and he had seen some really quite pickled looking brains in his days. That said, he had also seen some rather interesting looking brains too, for instance there was one time where he had had to weigh a brain that still had some shrapnel lodged within it from the war and there was the chap with another brain growing from the left side of his existing brain. Or the brain within a brain that was also packed nicely within a brain and then there was the woman with teeth and hair growing in the middle of her brain, which Mr Wilkomsir had said was the ladies twin. But all these thoughts of brains were not helping Clarence as he peered through the darkness. "Hello?" He called, grabbing the lamp from the desk as his skinny knees almost knocked together like a pair of lily white drumsticks. The floorboards creaked beneath his feet as he tiptoed his way down the darkened corridor towards the mortuary's cutting room. He could feel the chill of the tiled room as he approached and his lamp light flickered strange shapes either side of him like ghostly phantoms, chasing him and then falling behind with the flames every movement. The place was lit only by moonlight sneaking in through the raised narrow windows that lined the room, but as it cast a silver beam onto the freezers he noticed that chiller number eleven was wide open and the drawer had been pulled right out.

"Oh Gods no… Not the dead girl." He tried to puff himself out a little, but it was hard to look brave in a nightgown, "Who's there? We don't hold valuables here you know so you might as well go back home." He spoke in such a matter of fact tone that he could almost be mistaken for brave, but inside, Clarence was a quivering wreck of yellow belly in a nightgown. A tinkling noise stopped him fast, whatever it was was now directly behind him. He turned suddenly and held the lamp at arm's length. It cast a circular glow before the boy which seemed to just accentuate the darkness beyond the golden lamp light. "Hello?" He whispered, staring intently into the halo of light.

A smiling female face suddenly appeared from the blackness. "Hello." It said.

"AGH!" Squealed Clarence as he stumbled backwards, tripped over a trolley and spilling its contents of tools across the floor making a din that could wake the dead. "You… you… you're the dead girl."

She walked over to him with her hands out. "Please don't be frightened. I thought you liked me. You spoke to me so kindly before."

Clarence slid across the floor on his bottom. "That was before I knew you were alive… I mean dead…Get back I say… you… you Zombie."

The dead girl giggled, "I'm not a Zombie you silly boy."

"But you are dead?" Clarence's brow furrowed as he tried to make sense of this young dead girl in her new state of living undeadness.

She looked around her and giggled, "Well I am in a Morgue so I imagine I must be, yes."

He stood up cautiously and straightened his night gown, "I'm Clarence." Said Clarence. "Clarence Bunn."

The girl giggled again, "I know, you told me earlier."

"But you were… are dead! Oh I don't

understand. This must all be a silly dream."

The girl reached forward and pinched Clarence on the arm.

"Ouch, that hurt… You pinched me."

"Well then you're not asleep are you Clarence Bunn?" She suddenly coughed and some murky water bubbled out of her mouth onto the floor. "Oops, Sorry," said the girl, sheepishly looking at the floor and wiping her mouth.

"That's ok… I… I think," said the boy as he scratched his head, "I guess that's sea water?"

"Yes it is… My body must have drowned after I hit the water." She giggled again.

Clarence still felt very uneasy, this was the first time a dead body had spoken back to him or let alone pinched him. "I… Urm, I don't think I caught your name."

"That's because I never told you," she clasped her hands together and bashfully held them down, "I'm Kelly."

"And my name's…" He realised the foolishness that was about to spill out from his mouth and stopped himself just in time. "…Oh, I told you that already." He looked at her white shroud and shamefully realised they were almost in the same outfit. "You must be cold. I… urm… have some clothes you may borrow. I mean, that's if you would like to borrow them that is." He pursed his lips tightly and tried desperately to shut himself up before anymore nonsense bumbled out. He was never any good with general conversation let alone with a girl, albeit a dead one, but a girl non the less and that was the worst thing ever for him. He would always gibber and stammer when he had to speak with a female and this beautiful dead girl situation was not helping matters at all. If only she had just stayed dead he thought, then this conversation would be so much less stressful.

"That would be very sweet of you Clarence Bunn thank you… You are a true gentleman…" She curtsied at him, "Although you did call me a zombie." She poked his chest and Clarence jumped back a little.

"My goodness you are freezing cold," said the young man as he rubbed his chest.

"Well I am dead Clarence," giggled Kelly.

"I should show you my room, I mean to show you my clothes… to borrow I mean." He quickly turned and led her out of the Morgue. "Do you even feel the cold? I mean seeing as you are dead and all?"

"A little I suppose, yes."

The warm air caressed their faces as the door opened to Clarence's room, "Here please, do sit down." He scrambled to clear some clothes from his bed. "Would you like a hot drink?"

"Oh Clarence thank you but if I drink anything I fear it will come straight back up."

Clarence sat on the desk opposite Kelly. He stared at the girl in wonder. She was so pretty and alive but dead, how very strange he thought. "I would like to know… if it would be ok with you, how you… well… how you died?"

Kelly looked at the floor with a solemn expression on her face. "I wish I could tell you Clarence Bunn but I'm unable, you see I'm forbidden to tell anyone who I really am and besides," she looked Clarence deep in the eye, "You see the last thing I remember is arguing with my father and then lots of cold sea water and then, well, waking up in your morgue with you."

She sniffed and looked at Clarence. "I can't even cry. I have no tears."

Clarence instinctively leapt up and sat next to her, placing an arm round her shoulder, "It's ok Kelly." He suddenly realised the predicament he was in. He had a girl in his room for the first time ever and his arm was round her shoulder and if that was not enough for the poor boys hormones to contend with, she was now snuggling up to him. "Urm… just let it out and we will find out what happened," stuttered

Clarence as he stared uncomfortably at his warped reflection in the metal tea pot. The girl felt as dead as any other corpse that Clarence had met, she was cold and had that heavy feeling about her, but something else was there, something that the boy could not quite put his finger on. Even that deadness of the eyes seemed to twinkle out a life of some sort. Something behind the glassy dead look that was almost alive but more than dead!

"Bunn? What in the?… By gods you've gone too far now."

Clarence looked up in shock at a very red faced Mr. Wilkomsir standing in the door way of his room. "This is not what it looks like sir… I'm… this is."

Kelly interrupted, "I'm Kelly. You must be Mr. Wilkomsir."

The old man pointed and his jaw fell open, "But you… you're dead!"

She stood and beamed a smile, "Hello."

"Auk!" Muttered Mr. Wilkomsir as he fainted.

The popping and crackling of the fire welcomed Mr. Wilkomsir out of his unconscious slumber and into the nice warm, familiar surroundings of his office. A lone lamp burning in the corner gave the room its comfortable ambience. "Auk Clarence I had the funniest dream about you and the dead girl in number eleven."

 "It's ok Mr. Wilkomsir… it really is ok."

 "What happened to me? Was it a funny bottle of whisky? I never should've trusted that crazy looking old man Busby and his cheap moonshine." The Scotsman rubbed his head and sat forward.

 The boy fiddled uncomfortably with his shirt buttons. "Well… I'm not sure how to explain this but. Well the dead girl is not actually dead."

 Mr. Wilkomsir immediately leapt up from the sofa, "So it was real? I didn't dream it?"

 Clarence scrunched up his face and stepped aside, "This is the dead… urm, Kelly."

 The big man cautiously stepped forward and held out a hand, pressing a finger against her forehead. "Well she feels dead, and she certainly looks dead… but why on earth is she no' dead?"

 Kelly smiled at the large man, "But I am dead Mr. Wilkomsir."

 "Auk no ya cannae be dead but no', It's just no' right."

 Clarence could always tell when Mr. Wilkomsir was anxious because he would suddenly become very much more Scottish than usual, as if he had forgotten himself in the moment and went back to his roots in the highlands. "Well she is sir. We don't know why or how but she just is."

"Well come Monday we can get this all cleared up boy?"

"But don't you think we should just keep her here with us? She could help in the mortuary? She knows all about the dead, I mean, she is dead after all. Let's give her a chance?"

Mr. Wilkomsir leaned in close to Clarence, "Dear gods' boy... This isn't right by any stretch of anyone's imagination, we can't just keep her, she's no' a wee rabbit or puppy ya found on the street... I mean when was the last time you saw a walking deaden? You heard of zombies have ya no'?"

"But sir she's not a zombie. She just happens to be a living dead person."

"And they're no' one and the same thing? Who's to say she's no' sizing us up right now, contemplating which one of our brains to eat first."

Clarence looked at Kelly as she rearranged some flowers in their vase. She was no flesh eating zombie, she was just an unfortunate and, if Clarence did say so, rather pretty soul that had perhaps not quite died in the time honoured tradition of staying dead. "No, I won't believe it of her Mr. Wilkomsir. I just won't."

"Well I think La Douche will decide that on Monday… If she hasn't killed you by then and eaten ya foolish wee brain out." Wilkomsir took a long, despairing look at the boy, "Right, I need a drink… You tidy up and I'll see you." He looked at his pocket watch; it was half past three Saturday morning, "Sometime on Monday afternoon." And with that Mr. Wilkomsir staggered out of the office, muttering profanities' and making it very obvious that he did not approve of the dead girl.

Kelly stared at Clarence as he snored in his bed, he looked so peaceful as he slept and she wished she could just lay next to her new friend and sleep too, but she couldn't and that upset her. He had been so very kind to her and considering his initial fear and apprehension, he had been really rather understanding of the whole deathly situation. She smiled as she ran her fingers through his hair, "Thank you Clarence Bunn," whispered the dead girl. She backed away towards the door and as the clock chimed 5 in the morning she sighed, "I'll be back very soon."

Clarence muttered something about the dawning of the badgers, grinned and then hugged his pillow.

The streets were quiet at this time of day and a heavy frost had covered anything cold enough for it to stick too. There was a creak as the large metal graveyard gate swung open and Kelly breathed in the air through her nose, closing her eyes for a moment to take in that familiar smell, of death. She could feel something pulling gently at her innards like a fish hook and so she stepped forward on the hallowed soil while the essence of death moved through her like an old familiar friend speaking into her thoughts; leading her between the graves and tombs that stood proud around her like buildings. She could feel restful spirits wafting through the air around her, caressing her skin and her thoughts as an immense feeling of peace washed over her.
Suddenly a noise broke her concentration and she wandered between the large statues and tombstones, giggling at a stone effigy of the grim reaper, its skeletal face looking down upon the grave it stood over like a guardian of the corpse within. There was another sound, someone was talking and as she peered

behind the reaper Kelly saw five teenagers sitting in a circle on the ground. They appeared to be playing a board game with letters and numbers, "Hello," she said, as a synchronised scream came from the group, seeing Kelly's deathly pale face peering from behind the statue. "I'm Kelly," she continued, to the startled teens.

"Are you a thpirit?" Lisped a very gaunt looking young man dressed in clothes a hundred years his senior. He stood and waved his arms about, "Twas we, the Gothic children whom did conjure you oh thpirit." His lacy cuffs swished around as he twiddled his fingers in Kellys face.

She bit her lip and tried not to laugh at the boy, "No, I'm not a spirit if that's what you were implying, I'm a girl and my name is Kelly."

"Oh! Well you look rather pale, and deathly, just like a thpirit!" The boy pondered for a moment then continued, "Well I'm Colin, but they call me Vlad." He lowered his arms and looked back round at his friends, "Who wasn't bloody conthentrating then?" There was a collective mumble around the little group but no one confessed. "Wath it you Edwin?"

A ginger haired boy sniffed and pushed his glasses up the bridge of his nose, "Not me, I was trying to connect to the spirits, honest."

"Perhaps the spirits are all at rest here," suggested Kelly, trying to help, "Just a thought," she said with a wink.

"Oh?" Said the boy again. "Are you some thort of expert then?"

Kelly smiled knowingly, "I imagine I am yes… So what are you supposed to be? Are you some kind of society?"

"Yeth, of a fashion." Vlad puffed out his chest, placed his hands on his hips and stared off into the distance. "We are the Ashwood Gothicth and we like to thpend our eveningth in the graveyard talking to the dead."

Kelly laughed to herself, if only they knew, "And do they ever answer you?"

"Well not really, but Peregrine there had a nose bleed one night and we indubitably put it down to the thpirits!"

As the boy said the word 'spirits' he wiggled his fingers and raised his eyebrows in an attempt to look spooky, but Kelly could not take the lisping teen seriously and especially in that outfit. "So you're?"

"Vampireth!"

"Oh, the old authentic type of Vampires?"

Vlad looked a little uncomfortable and a couple of the others fidgeted in their costumes too,

"Yeth, authentic clothing like the original Vampires of the bygone dayth of yore."

"And are they your own teeth?"

Vlad swiftly spat the false teeth into his handkerchief, "Urm… Well no, not really but I think it adds to the ambiance."

Kelly noticed the boy's lisp had vanished with his teeth but chose not to mention this in an attempt to spare any further embarrassment to the poor child. "Well I think you all look rather good, in an authentic, Vampirey kind of way." She smiled and felt a little sorry for the now embarrassed looking teenagers. All of a sudden a cold wind whipped through the cemetery and blew past Kelly and the others; it brought with it a haunting howl.

The youngest member of the Ashwood Gothics stood quickly, "What the bloody hell was that?" She squealed.

"Oh it was just the wind," said Kelly as another gust blew her auburn hair across her face, but this time the sound of a moan echoed around the tombstones. "Ok maybe it's NOT just the wind then."

"Nice to have met you," said Vlad as he jumped over a gravestone and out of the graveyard, swiftly followed by the rest of the Ashwood Gothics.

The moaning continued and as Kelly's eyes adjusted to the darkness she could make out a figure limping through the misty cemetery, it's gangly arms waving around like some kind of grizzly ghoul trying to keep its balance "Clarence? Is that you?" She giggled.

"I fell in a bloody hole," hollered the lad as he limped through the mist, "Who were you talking to?"

"Oh, they were just some Vampires."

Clarence raised a questioning eyebrow but said no more about it. "What on earth are you doing in a cemetery? Is it because…?" He stopped himself from asking the obvious question and felt uncomfortable for merely suggesting it in his head.

"Were you about to say because I'm dead?"

"Yes, I was just about to say that… I'm sorry, it's just that well, I've never met a dead girl before and I'm a little lost for dead etiquette."

Kelly took his arm and smiled sweetly at the skinny lad, "Walk me home Clarence Bunn."

A kerfuffle of kidnappers
The Sunday morning church bells rang out across the city, calling the people to prayer and waking Clarence from a very deep sleep indeed. He had been dreaming about some rather nasty fellows in bowler hats who had taken a disliking to some pastries that he had made. His dreams were always very odd though, as he slid his bruised legs out of the bed, rubbed the pinch bruise on his arm, yawned and focused his blurry eyes on Kelly.

"Good morning sleepy head." She sat on the chest of drawers smiling at him.

Clarence looked at the girl and noticed that she was wearing one of his shirts, tucked into a pair of his trousers. She looked like an angel sat there and he beamed a smile back at her, "What time is it?"

"It's nine and I've made you some tea."

"Thank you Kelly," he sat up and stretched, "How did you sleep?"

"Oh I don't sleep, or rather I just don't need to sleep… It's much like the eating and drinking thing… Another occupational hazard I have in this world I suppose."

Clarence frowned, Kelly was talking about being dead as if she was experienced at it, but she had only been found two days ago. He reached for his cup, slurped at it and tried to forget the thought.. "I'm worried for tomorrow," he suddenly stammered.

"Why ever so Clarence?"

"I think La Douche will want to take you away from me."

"Clarence Bunn? You're talking as if we're courting?"

Clarence blushed furiously, "I didn't mean… Well…"

"And while we are on the subject, did you mean what you said yesterday?"

"About what?" Clarences face was just cooling back down but he feared the worst was about to happen.

"You told Mr. Wilkomsir that you thought I was pretty… twice as I recall!"

Clarences' face now reached subnormal temperatures and he thought that his head would surely pop with overheated embarrassment, "I… Umm," he attempted.

"No one has ever said that to me before and It made something happen in my chest."

"Your heart? Did it beat?"

Kelly giggled, "No, I'm dead you silly boy, but it did feel awfully funny."

Clarence suddenly looked stern and sincere, "I

think we should run away… Today."

Kelly frowned, "Oh Clarence, don't be silly."

"I mean it Kelly, he stood abruptly, "We should get away from here… You're not safe and I have the most awful feeling."

"But where would we run to?"

"I don't know but… Well it's just tomorrow."

"Oh La Douche?"

"Yes, I've heard things about him, that he performs experiments on people, you know, like those from the freak shows."

Kelly stood up, "I'm not a freak Clarence but if that's what you think then I'll just go." She barged past him but Clarence grabbed her arm.

"That isn't what I meant Kelly, I merely suggested that you are… Well a bit… unique?"

Kelly looked down in an attempt to hide her smile, "Oh Clarence, you really are a gentleman." She reached forward and kissed him on the cheek. "But all will be fine I'm sure."

Although her lips were ice cold, Clarence felt a certain warmth to them, from the soul maybe, that was if she had one at all he though. "I will not let them take you from me and I will let nothing happen to you… I promise."

The dead girl flung her arms round him and squeezed him tightly. It was an odd kind of embrace because Clarence was unsure of what to do, "I've never been hugged before," he mumbled.

Kelly looked up at him and frowned, "What, never ever? Not even by your parents?"

"I never knew my mother and father lost me in a bet when I was three years old."

Kelly squeezed him tighter, "Hug me back Clarence," she whispered.

He placed his reluctant arms around the girl's shoulders and stared uncomfortably ahead.

"Tighter Clarence," said Kelly in a slightly raised voice.

"He obediently squeezed."

"Mmm that's nice," she whispered.

"It is?"

"Yes Clarence. It is. Now Shush."

He smiled at the oddness of it all. Here he was having his first ever hug and it was with a dead girl.

"Clarence? Do you have any other family?"

"I was told I have an uncle, Cecil I think, but nobody knows where he is, I imagine he is just like my father, an old soak and gambler."

"Well you have me Clarence, I'll be your family for now, if you want?"

Everything seemed to be travelling at such a vast rate in the young man's head. Just this time yesterday he was putting lipstick on a little old, dead Mrs. Scrubshole and now… Now he was in an embrace with a walking, talking beautiful corpse.

Suddenly a heavy thud and ping of the front door ruined the moment.

"The door? It must be Mr. Wilkomsir… But it's only Sunday." Clarence hurried to the foyer and saw Mr. Wilkomsir standing with two other gentlemen.

"Bunn, I'm sorry boy but I had to do it."

The two men rushed forward, one grabbed Clarence while the other went out the back to find Kelly. He heard her screaming and tried to escape but the man holding him was far too strong. "Unhand me at once…What is this?" He looked to his boss for help, "Mr. Wilkomsir?"

"I'm sorry Clarence, I had no other choice." He bowed his head in shame and moved aside as another man walked in.

He was the most elegant of gentlemen in a dark blue suit, top hat with goggles and a silver topped cane.

"La Douche?" He struggled in the man's clutches and clenched his fists while his legs wiggled frantically in the air. Another first was happening to Clarence and it was the feeling of rage.

"Oui, and you must be Monsieur Bunn no? I

am 'ere for the dead girl nothing more." He looked past Clarence and widened his eyes, causing his monocle to fall from his cheek. "And 'ere she is." La Douche was the head of Anthropology and forensic sciences at one of Frances most illustrious universities. He had studied the human body for so many years that he could forget the exact date in which studies commenced but this was something that the world had never seen, a corpse that walked and talked like the living.

Kelly was being carried over the shoulder of the second large henchman, "Let me go!" She screamed, as she punched and kicked the man. "Clarence, help me," she called.

"What will it be Monsieur Bunn." La Douche twisted his cane, revealing the neck of a sword, "The last thing I want is to hurt you young Clarence, or anyone for that matter, that is not the kind of man I am, but if I must then so be it. I will take the girl now for all of our sakes; but she will be safe with me, I promise you this." He smiled and stroked his little white goatee beard and taped the cane on the floor, "We leave now."

Clarence watched as Kelly was carried from the building, her terrified eyes staring straight at his. "No! Kelly." He lurched free from the grip of the henchman but there was a sudden and very heavy pain in his head, and everything went black and swimmy for a moment.

"Stay down fella, else my Billy clubs' gonna be smashing your skull in… Alright?"

Clarence lay on the floor trembling with his hands over the now throbbing area on the back of his head, he could smell his own blood as his eyes blurred with tears, "Ye… Yes sir."

"Good boy." The henchman stepped over poor Clarence and followed his companion to a large, richly gilded carriage that waited on the cobbles.

The boy stood up, slowly catching his bearings and then ran to the street to see the carriage drive off down the road, he looked at Mr. Wilkomsir, "How could you?"

"She wasn't normal boy."

"No she wasn't, you're right… She was very special… Unique in fact."

"Ay but I think she was a brain eating zombie."

"Well she did not eat mine last night, in fact she made me a very nice cup of tea, in my favourite cup too."

"Well you were lucky this time."

"Lucky? I was lucky to have found her. She was the only worthwhile thing to ever happen in my life."

"Ah you only met her yesterday for god's sake," Growled the Scotsman as he raised his arms in despair.

Clarence stomped past, back in doors and through to the still disheveled morgue. He felt his heart beating like one of those steam trains and for the first time in his life he felt brave.
"Yes I did and that was enough time for me to realise." The mortuary book was still open and Clarence scratched a pen across the last entry and in big letters he wrote "ALIVE!".
He turned and stomped back out to the cobbled street.

"What are you doing boy? Where are you going?"

Clarence stopped, raised his hand and shouted, "Taxi!"

___Flight or fight?___
 The Frenchman sat with both hands on his cane and stared thoughtfully at the dead girl before him as the carriage thundered through the city. "You are an enigma mademoiselle, but I François La Douche intend to crack your little code and find out how you work. Tick-tock." He laughed as he moved the cane like the pendulum in a grandfather clock. He was indeed a man of science and one who would, if presented with the correct tools, take apart the very universe to see how it worked if he could. But the big Scottish mortician would only have the worst said of La Douche, which was unfair as the Frenchman was also very keen to learn how life worked and although his reputation for macabre experiments followed him like a bad smell, he was not a bad person at all, he was merely a scientist in search of knowledge and the truth. He was a great man, a genius but even geniuses still needed to learn and if his studies led him to unusual measures, which in fact they quite often did, then he would take those measures.

 "Why do you want me so much? I'm only a girl," whimpered Kelly.

 La Douche leaned forward, "Oui, but not like

any other girl are you? You started as a mere dead girl and I wished only to find how you met that end, but now…" The Frenchman mused for a moment before continuing, "You are dead and yet alive at the same time and that, is enchanting."

Kelly chewed the inside of her lip and remembered what Clarence had said just the night before about La Douche. "Where are you taking me?" She pleaded.

"We are going to my laboratory. That is all. I just want to know your secrets. Just with a little drop of blood here and there."

"You really do not want to know my secrets Mr. La Douche, trust me, you would not understand."

The Frenchman sat back and peered out from behind the little curtain that covered the window, "Young lady there are many things in this world that do not wish to be known but alas, there are always men such as myself who seek the unknown. We dig deep until the answers are revealed for the world to see. Sometimes they hurt us but that is life no? Surely even a painful truth is better than a lie? And maybe I would not understand your secrets but that is my job, to seek the unknown."

All of a sudden a large crash brought the carriage to a halt and a great commotion could be heard outside.

La Douche looked at his henchman, "William. Go and see why we have stopped."

"Right you are boss," said the burly man as he pulled out the Billy club, slapped it into his palm and jumped from the cab.

La Douche peered around the little curtain again and bumped his cane onto the floor, "Excuse me just one moment. It looks as if I must do everything myself." He too, then jumped down from the carriage, slamming the door behind him.

"What is this?" A circus wagon was blocking their path and a tall skinny man in bright red tails and top hat stood stroking one of the scientists horses. At his feet were the two henchmen of La Douche.

"Sir. I am ring master Maurice Turnbuckle and I understand you have a very special object with you?"

"I do not know of what you are talking Monsieur I am sure. But you will remove your wagon this instant." He drew the sword from his cane, "Otherwise I shall run you through."

"I am sure we can get around this without it resorting to violence sir."

La Douche looked at his unconscious henchmen, "It would appear that the situation has already escalated to a violent outcome, and by your own hand Monsieur." He held out his sword, "You know I am one of the finest swordsmen in all of France?"

The ring master unwound his whip, twisted his curly moustache with a gloved hand and smirked. "My word. You are a rather over confident chap aren't you?"

"No sir I am just better than a lowly circus performer."

Turnbuckle wound his whip back up again and bowed. "I have no time for this today sir, but perhaps another time and place yes?"

La Douche swished his sword about the place and laughed, "You are a coward no?"

"No, just savvy." Suddenly a large club hit La Douche on the back of the head, rendering him unconscious. "Strongman, if you will?" He continued.

The carriage door fell to the ground and a giant man in a leopard skin leotard stood with his arms folded. In front of him was Turnbuckle.

"My dear girl. I am here to rescue you from a terrible fate."

Kelly frowned, "But who are you?"

"Oh I must apologise for my impertinence."

Removing his hat the ring master took a large bow. "I am Maurice Turnbuckle, ring master of the Turnbuckle travelling circus of the macabre, at your service."

"But how did you know? I mean how did you find out about me?"

Maurice climbed into the carriage and sat opposite Kelly, "My dear child. I make it my business to know such things… Besides I have a Clown with a certain talent for reading the future through the Tarot cards." He smirked an evil smirk and widened his dark ringed eyes.

Kelly felt a wave of panic in her gut, either that or it was some left over sea water from when she had drowned. Either way, the feeling was rather unpleasant. "Tarot?"

"Yes. You have heard of this arcane magic before I assume?"

"Did they mention Clarence?"

"There was no mention of a Clarence. Is he a friend of yours? Perhaps you lover?" His smirk appeared almost filthy as he said the words, his mind seemingly wanting to know any dirty or sordid secrets that the girl may keep hidden.

Kelly wished she had tears because right now she just wanted to cry. "No he is not. He is my friend." She looked at the floor guiltily trying to hide the lie she had just told.

"Then may I enquire as to whom this Clarence is?"

"No you may not but if I may sir, just tell me wh cards were dealt?"

"Funny you should ask such a thing. The usual cards came up but every time the cards were dealt, Death would be first. Even when the card was removed from the deck, it would mysteriously reappear… Strange but then you are, after all, dead are you not?.."

"Yes I am."

Maurice leaned forward, reached out a hand and smiled a foul grin "So if you would let me escort you from here so we might make you safer?"

Kelly looked out of the little back window of the carriage. No Clarence to the rescue she thought and after he had promised to look after her. She looked at the man with his curled moustache, black eyeliner and sinister smile. What would be in store for her if she were to go with him? Kelly felt her hand move instinctively onto the opposite door handle, it clicked down and she shook her head, "I'm sorry, I just cannot. Not today. Not ever." And with that, the door opened. Turnbuckle grabbed at the girl but missed as she leaped from the carriage and ran into the darkness.

"Curses!" He shouted as the first snowflakes of winter fell onto his black leather glove. He leaned from the carriage door like a creepy, slender spider. "I will find you girl. You are a little money tree and I shall pluck your leaves until nothing remains but my swollen pockets." He turned and hit the strongman with the handle of his whip before stomping back to his carriage.

To the circus!

A very worried Clarence hung from the carriage window as the taxi sped through the streets. "Please Mr. Leech, you must drive faster if you can. I must find Kelly."

"Right you are Mr. Bunn. Ol' Nelly's doin' her best."

The cab driver took a corner on two wheels sending sparks flying into the air as metal scraped upon stone. "Wooo there Nelly." The driver called to his horse.

"Whatever is the matter Mr. Leech? Why are we stopping?"

"There's a road block Mr. Bunn." He jumped down and patted his old nag on the neck. "Shh Nelly," he said as he fed the horse some sugar cubes.

Clarence followed Mr. Leech and stood next to him. The pair marvelled at the sight of police and carriages. "What do we do now?"

"I'm afraid it's out of my hands now sir. As Mrs. Leech would say, it's all in the hands of them there gods. And by jiminy there's a lot of nonsense to be fixing here young sir. All this traffic and people is going to take all day to sort out by my reckonings."

Clarence looked at the scene. He could see

the large carriage that had taken Kelly and there was Monsieur La Douche rubbing his head as he spoke to a policeman. He ran forward, through the crowds and to the Frenchman. "Where is she you… you brute."

"Monsieur Bunn. You would not believe. The dead girl has disappeared into the night like a bird."

"What have you done?"

He laughed as he placed his top hat back onto his head, "Let us just say, it is not only we, who seek the girl." He pointed at the huge circus wagons as they passed. "Le Cirque."

"Oh my."

"Oui Clarence. Perhaps you will end this escapade now? It is after all futile."

Young Clarence felt his heart sink as he backed away through the crowd. His focus was on La Douche and his moving lips as everything around him blurred into insignificance.

"Mr. Bunn?"

Clarence turned to see the round, red face of Mr. Leech the cab driver beaming at him. His bowler hat in his hands against his chest, "Sir?"

Clarence sniffed, "What do I do now?"

"You come back with me sir. Mrs. Leech would love to see you."

"Thank you Mr. Leech. You are a good friend."
 But that evening Clarence sat silently at the Leech's dining table. He stared at the soup in front of him, untouched and growing cold. He heard nothing but muffled sounds as Mrs. Leech busied around, fussing and talking in her busy, bumbling manner. Only the sound of Kelly screaming for help could be heard in his mind as she was carried away. It haunted his memory like a continuous waking nightmare, but furthermore was the shame that he was unable to save her as he had promised and that tore at his heart like shameful meat hooks. A broken promise was as good as lie in his books and Clarence certainly was not a liar, perhaps a coward or a fool but he never lied.
 Mr. Leech sat down in front of him, "Young Mr. Clarence sir. Mrs. Leech and I were wondering if you would like to lodge here? We understand that you can't go back to the mortuary so please, it would be our pleasure."
 "I would yes… thank you."
 "I'll make you a bed up in the roof then." Said Mrs. Leech as she made her way up the stairs with a large pile of linen already expectantly in her arms.
 Clarence loved Mr. and Mrs. Leech. They had always been so good to him and were such a

lovely, homely couple. Mr. was an old, round man with a heart of gold that matched his big, jolly red face that shone out through large white mutton chop sideburns. His wife was of equal size and shape and just as jolly as her husband. Clarence saw them as close to family as he had got and he knew they would do anything in their power for him.

"Mr. Clarence. Are you not curious as to the circus that the Frenchman mentioned? It's just that, well Mrs. Leech does so love the circus, all those funny folks with their odd knobbly bits and beardy ladies and the like, says it reminds her of her old aunt Lucy, she had a beard, down to her chest it was." Mr. Leech reached across the table and placed a comforting hand on Clarence' arm, "And besides, you might find a clue or two." He winked and smiled a knowing smile.

Clarence nodded, "It would be a good start Mr. Leech," he looked at his pocket watch, "We might just make the evening show."

The snow was now an inch deep on the ground as the trio made their way towards the sound of the circus. Mr. and Mrs. Leech bumbled along, arms linked like excited children.

"Oh husband, you are romantic taking me out

to the circus."

"Anything for you my little love..." He chuffed.

Clarence bounded ahead, his mission clear, to find someone, anyone with information about Kelly.

The sound from the circus filled the air, jolly people and screaming children mixed with the steam powered organ that played along with the merry-go-round. Clarence sniffed in the smell of sausages and candy floss as he eyed the tents suspiciously. Everything surrounded the big top like planets around a big red and white striped sun. Anyone of the smaller tents could be holding Kelly and he looked back at Mr. Leech who nodded back at him knowingly. "Right!" He said sternly. He had never felt as determined in his life as he did when he pulled open the first tent and marched in.

"Wadda ya want? Hic." A Clown sat in the darkness at the back of the tent. A small Jack Russell terrier sat on his lap and snarled, it wore a tiny, pointed red hat that was cocked to the side. "It says I'm shut on the door doesn't it? Can't ya read?"

Clarence checked, "Urm… There is no sign sir. I'm here looking for…"

"Shh!" Said the Clown as he hovered his hand over the deck of cards. "These bloody cards are gonna be the death of me. Hic." He swigged from a bottle and seemed to phase out for a moment. "Well? Sit ya'self down boy we haven't got all bloody day," slurred the costumed drunkard.

 Clarence sat opposite the Clown and even with a table between them he could smell the brewery contained within the old Clowns breath. He was a stereotypical looking Clown with a stripy, frilled costume and big orange wig that was slightly off centre, much like the dogs little hat. But there was something a little, if not really rather grubby about this particular funny man, something that didn't quite tick all the boxes associated with a Clown and Clarence felt that it went further than just the smell of booze.

 "Well pick a bloody card then," shouted the Clown impatiently.

 The young man picked a card obediently and flipped it, face up on the table, it was death.

 "Christ! It's always death!" Roared the Clown as he slammed his head onto the table, there was a pause before a deep snore rumbled from the clown until he suddenly jerked back up and leaned over at the young man with the death card stuck to his greasy forehead. "I shuffled these eighty times!" He held up three fingers and repeated himself, "eighty bloody times, and still death… What do you want and why have you brought this with you?" He noticed the card and swiftly removed it, hoping that Clarence hadn't seen the obviously and rather awkwardly placed Tarot.

Clarence leaned away from the toxic breath as his left eye quivered from the fumes, "I want to find a girl."

The Clown winked and leaned back, folding his arms, "Don't we all. But what do you REALLY want?" He wave a hand over the deck almost majestically, trying to conjure up a feeling of mystery, but failing miserably.

"No. That's it sir… I mean I'm looking for a particular girl. She's dead."

The Clown stood suddenly and gasped, sending his little terrier flying across the tent with a yelp. "DEATH!" He pointed a trembling finger of blame at Clarence. "It's you… Well, not YOU so to speak, because YOU'RE clearly not the Grimm Reaper and it's actually the girl I'm referring to, unless you are a girl, but still." He paused to catch his breath, picked up the dog and placed him back under his arm. "And Mr. Fluffles agrees, don't ya boy?" The little white and brown terrier growled at Clarence, "See, the dog's a small... urm, I mean a large!"

He pondered on the words for a moment and then continued, "the dogs a medium." A huge smile beamed across the Clown's face, expecting a laugh, but there was no sound of drums, and certainly no symbol to end the gag, there was just the sound of a lone cricket outside, chirping to itself, "Tough audience tonight ay Fluffles?" He said, looking at the dog.

Clarence placed his palms on the table and made his most pitiful and desperate face at the clown. "So do you know anything about Kelly?"

"Who?"

"Kelly."

"The dead girl?"

"Yes."

"Hmm!" Pondered the Clown. "Yes I do. I tell you one thing though…" He removed a hip flask within his jacket and glugged on the bottle until it was empty. "She's not the sausage." Mr. Fluffles looked up and made a confused squeak sound.

"Sausage?"

"No she is not here at… at this place that is the circus and that's for certain… or the freak show as it happens. No, no she isn't there... But…" The Clown paused for much longer than was necessary, and appeared to not be breathing.

"But what sir? Mr clown? Please, where is

she?" Clarence was becoming desperate now and the more drunk the Clown became was time wasted in the hunt for Kelly. "Please Mr. Clown you must help me… Please."

The Clown slumped back onto the chair, breathed out deeply and then stared almost sober at the lad. "I used to be called Mr. Giggles you know, Quietus Giggles. That was before I lost my life in the bottom of a bottle. Now… well now there are no more giggles. There is just an angry drunk man in a costume." He squeaked his nose and threw it for Mr. Fluffles. "I know the feeling of desperation my boy. I feel it every day of my life. Sometimes I wonder whether the world would notice if an old drunken Clown just disappeared." He pulled the stub of a cigar from behind his ear and lit it with a match struck from his stubbly chin, sending the smell of singed grease paint into the air and up Clarence's nose making him cough. "But then I look at Mr. Fluffles there and I say yes, yes Clown you old codger, that's why you're still here, in this unforgiving place." He sniffed and wiped his runny nose across the grease paint of his cheek.

"Oh my," said Clarence, pulling his handkerchief from his pocket and passing it across the table, "That is sad sir… Mr. Clown sir. But why are you telling me this?"

The clown pushed the handkerchief back to Clarence and proceeded to pull a string of multicoloured handkerchiefs from his sleeve, there seemed an almost endless line of colourful material, until he finally pulled out a rubber chicken. "I'm telling you because I feel there's something about you. Clarice?" He squeezed the chicken and threw it over his shoulder.

"It's Clarence." Said Clarence.

"Yes, yes it is, and I feel your pain. But you know that when I think of your girl." He phased out again into a drunken but strangely focused state. "All I see is darkness. The other side. I see death."

The boy leaned over the table, "She's dead?"

"Well yes but we knew that." He winked in an oddly, eye twitchingly slurred manner.

"You know what I mean Mr. Clown?"

The Clown smiled a drunken smile that cracked the paint on his cheeks. "I know what you mean, but I am a Clown and jokes are, well, they're kinda what I do… But she is lost. In the city. Hic!" He gasped suddenly, "Oh dear. That's not the place for a lady." Then his head slammed against the table again in a drunken, trance like state, releasing another almighty snore.

"Clown? Mr Clown?" Clarence stood up and shook the Clowns shoulder, but nothing apart from a grunt left the body. "Great. Now I will never know what he meant. The city is far to big."

The Clown suddenly sat bolt up right, startling Clarence. His eyes rolling around like spinning tops as he pointed at the boy. "Ay clear off. I'm closed… Oh Clarkfield, you're back, or are you still here?" He puffed out his cheeks and blew out some rancid, smokey alcohol breath.

"It's Clarence."

"Yes, apparently so, well done. Look I felt what you felt and it reminded me of what I lost a long, long time ago and, well…" He phased out one last time. "Go to the city slums and you will find your dead girl. Beware the pair in bowler hats as you will not see their faces til it's too late. Good luck Charlie."

"Thank you, and my name's Clarence." He reached the tent door and stopped as a thought hit him and he turned back around, "May I ask a question?"

"Yes dear." Said the drunkard Clown.

"Do you drink embalming fluids?"

Pennys Den.
By now the snow was getting heavy and deep and Kelly was panicking as the hour was late. The city was a great big place and she was not used to being on the streets of such a vast place and since the events of the day so far, her nerves were in shreds. There were lots of people around still but in particular there were two men. Their bowler hats cocked forward and scarves obscured there features. The pair had been following for a while and it was frightening her. Suddenly she noticed a small group of ladies in a doorway; perhaps they were from the women's institute she thought.

"Excuse me," said Kelly.

The three women all turned and the one nearest to her puffed on a cigarette. "Ello' ducks. You alright?" She screeched.

"I'm lost," whispered Kelly.

The second women nudged the third, "Aww poor little loves all lost Dolly, look."

"Ain't ya got nowhere to go sweet 'art?" Said the first.

"No I haven't and those men are following me too." She pointed to the men who seemed to vanish into the shadows as soon as they were seen.

"Ere' bugger off!" Shouted Dolly to the shadowy

characters.

"Well they ain't hangin' around now look. Go on wiv ya!" "Ere, what ya reckon on comin' back wiv us for some stew or sumfink. You'll catch ya death out ere." Said the first woman.

Kelly smiled at the women. "I think I may have done already thank you."

The ladies were all very glamorous, dressed up with little umbrellas and fascinators, lots of makeup and they all smelled heavily of perfume. They huddled round Kelly like a bunch of mother hens as she walked down the road with them.

"What's ya name love?" Said the first woman.

"Oh my name is Kelly. I'm pleased to meet you."

"And you darlin'. This is Dolly Goodlove. She's Polly Gripwell and I'm Molly Pulard."

As they turned a corner Kelly noticed a large, fancy looking building with lights and music and a big sign that read 'Penny's Den'. Kelly looked up at it, "Wow. What is this place?"

"Oh this is Madam Penny's place," said Molly.

Polly pushed in, "She's gonna love you. Sweet young fing and wiv all ya own teeth too."

Kelly smiled but felt a little uncomfortable as they fussed and fluffed at her hair as they entered the building. A young lady ran giggling up the stairs as an old man chased her with his shirt out. Kelly had never seen such a place but it was warm and it felt safer than the snowy streets outside, especially with those two men lurking about.

Suddenly two loud claps silenced the hall and the three women looked down and curtsied. Kelly looked up the stairs and there, gliding down the staircase like a ghost was a tall and incredibly beautiful woman in the most fantastic gown she had ever seen. Her tall hair was full of gems and with a ringlet at either side that dropped down over her defined cheek bones.

Kelly grabbed the sides of her trousers and curtsied too. It just seemed like the right thing to do at the time, like an instinctive knee bending reflex to authority, although she did feel a little silly doing so in a pair of gentlemen's trousers.

The woman stood and glared down at the Kelly and then with a lace gloved finger beneath Kelly's chin she moved the girls head from side to side.

"Hmm!" she said before shooing off the three others. She spoke in a deep but seductively Russian sounding voice. "I am Dreadful."

Kelly raised an eyebrow but the woman

continued.

"Penny Dreadful and I am the Madam here."

Kelly curtsied again and wondered what a Madam was, perhaps it was French for owner or something she thought, "My name is Kelly. And I am very…"

Madam Dreadful interrupted, "You are welcome."

Molly leaned in and whispered something to the proprietor and then scuttled off with a little wave at Kelly as she went.

"My girls say you are very sweet and that you are lost? Please, to my boudoir." She clicked her fingers and Kelly assumed that to mean follow which she obediently did.

The room was lavish with a little table in its centre. A small, balding man stood just by the door. He had a petrified expression on his face and a silver tray that held two glasses of something, golden and bubbly.

"Champaign?" Said the Madam as she waltzed into the room.

"Oh no, not for me I'm fine thank you very much, I REALLY don't drink… at all."

"Very well. Then please, sit down."

Kelly sat rather gingerly on the edge of a very white sofa and gazed in awe at the lady's private sitting room. It was decorated like a palace with a huge bed set to the back by the window. Perhaps it was an extravagant bed-sit thought Kelly.

"So," said Dreadful as she draped herself across a luxurious sofa with golden metal edging that looped high across the back into the shape of two swan heads facing one another. "Why are you running?"

Kelly gulped. "How? How did you know that?"

The butler lit the cigarette that was poked into the end of its long holder and Penny drew back on it. "Darling." The word rolled, like a purr across her tongue, extenuating the R's. I have seen many a young woman pass through here. Many have been in trouble of some kind." She smiled and tilted her head. "You are a pretty thing Kelly, but it is not love you run from is it."

Kelly blinked slowly and shook her head.

Penny continued, "Whatever trouble you run from, know that you will come to no harm here. Our business is frowned upon by some, but we look after our fellow woman."

"It's just that." Kelly thought very carefully about what she was about to say because only one person understood and that was Clarence, the rest wanted to either cut her up or exhibit her in a freak show. "Miss Dreadful, it's like this. I have people looking for me, wanting to kill me perhaps and I'm very afraid for my... urm... friend, Clarence."

"He is looking for you also yes?"

Kelly looked at the floor and sniffed, "I hope so."

"My child, if he is half the man I think you would choose then I believe he is out there right now, hunting for you like a passionate wolf." Growled Penny as she clutched her chest with clenched fists.

Ace!

Clarence's teeth chattered together as he pressed on through the night. The snow was deep now but continued to fall and it stuck to his coat, soaking freezing water in through the fibres, biting at his skin like chilling razor blades and turning his eyebrows white and rather comically thick with ice. "Bloody weather." He mumbled as a droplet of snot froze on impact with the icy air and pinched at his top lip.

Two men barged passed him and one looked back, "Watch where ya goin will ya." He hissed with a venomous tone as his companion grabbed his arm and pulled him back in the direction they walked.

"Sorry sir!" whispered Clarence sheepishly. He watched as they disappeared off into the blanket of white and shivered at the thought of them. He supposed that they would've probably been the type to be carrying a knife or something else because this part of the city was like that. Many a body had passed through the morgue from the city slums and the great percentage of its victims had met with a rather sinister end involving something spiky or heavy or both. It was jolly difficult to accurately measure a bludgeoned and broken head remembered Clarence as he sniffed and looked at the buildings of the street, fearing slightly for his own life. A combination of taverns and shops faced him as well as a large and very well lit building with men falling from its doors. At its front stood a small group of overly glamorous ladies basking in the red light of the door way, giggling and beckoning to passing cloaked gentlemen. A sign above them read 'Penny's Den' and it flickered with gas lit flames. "Perhaps…?" Clarence thought for a second then looked at the quiet looking pub on the corner. He could hear a folk band playing within, "Yes, that's more like it." And he trudged across the road.

 The place was cosy inside and a fire poppet and crackled well, heating the pub comfortably. Three men sat in the corner, one on guitar, one with a double bass and the other with an assortment of percussion instruments. A very large banner hung behind them that read, DEAD SET. Clarence perched himself at the bar and pondered on the name, it was an odd choice for a jolly folk band as most were called The Country Bumpkins or the Local Yokels or there was even that one time he had seen an all girl band called The Farmer Charmers, but these chaps appeared a little too morbid for their choice of music. He waved at the barman and chose to ignore the odd named musicians, "Excuse me sir, but do you have any rooms?" He called.

"Aye!" said the bar keep with a toothless, ginger beardy grin that seemed to fill the entire lower half of his face.

"Urm… May I have one then please?"

"Aye."

Clarence smiled at the cross eyed bartender and pushed two coins towards him, "Will this be enough?"

"Aye."

"What number room will it be sir?"

"Foive."

"Five?"

"Aye. Foive."

Clarence continued to smile at the man as he took the key from the bar and backed away. A hand suddenly dropped onto his shoulder and he turned round with a start to see the square jaw of a tall man in flying jacket and western style hat. Clarence assumed the man to be an American and he was right. "Hey buddy. Not many young people in this bar. Ya wanna come help me finish this bottle of whisky?" Twanged the Americans voice.

"Oh golly!" Said Clarence as he looked around

at the other patrons, all sat with a pint and sad expression. "Urm... well I don't usually but."
"Good. The name's Ace, Ace Franklin."
"And I'm Clarence, Clarence Bunn."
"Well it sure is swell to meet ya Clarence. Why don't ya sit down."

Clarence smiled sheepishly, "So what brings you to England then...urm... Ace?" Clarence pondered on the name for a moment. Why were English names never as exhilarating as the Americans. Ace, Hank and Chuck were a lot more fun than Wally, Willy or, well Clarence.

"I Gotta job with some millionaire. He wants me to fly his new-fangled airship. He's paying top dollar so hey, I ain't about to say no right?" He winked and smacked Clarence across the arm.

"No I guess not," murmured Clarence as Ace pushed a glass of brown cloudy liquid into his hand, "Oh well, chin chin then what?" And he placed the glass to his lips.

Half an hour later and the two men were in a state of blurry drunkenness and the conversation soon got onto the subject of girls.

"So Clarence. Ya got ya self a woman?"

Clarence blushed through his already alcohol fuelled redness. "Well there is one girl I like.

She is everything I could ever have, Hic, imagined in a woman. She's the prettiest thing I've ever seen…" He looked at the snow that still fell outside and his lip quivered. "…And she has skin as pure as that snow." He placed his chin onto his hands and sighed deeply.

"Ya sure got it bad there buddy?"

He nodded and swayed in his chair, "Yup. She's in the city somewhere and I intend very much to find her and proclaim my luff to her I do," he slurred.

"I like you Clarence. Most of you Brits ain't got time for a yank. But you? You're a good egg." He raised a glass and sunk the contents.

"I have too wee!" announced Clarence as he staggered to his feet and set off to the gents.

The door burst open and he stumbled to the trough with his head pressed against the wall for balance.

"Ello Clawence!" came a gruff voice from beside him.

Clarence rotated his head and looked at the man next to him. "Hello. Do I know you?"

The man had a face like a bag of very battered potatoes and appeared to be just as dirty as a newly dug up spud. "Oh no young man, you do not know me. But I know you." He smirked a turreted, brown toothed grin and puffed on the stub of a roll up cigarette which he grasped in his fingerless gloves.

Clarence sighed as his bladder emptied.

"I am in search of a certain dead girl?"

Clarence's bladder ceased emptying instantly. "You're what now?" Bumbled Clarence.

"You heard me Clawence. Where might we find said girl?"

"I have no idea who you mean. Perhaps you seek another young man called Clawence, I mean Clarence!?" He felt a body press up behind him and a blade press against his groin. He coughed, "I don't know where she is. Honestly… I… I have no idea sir." He felt the alcoholic feeling drain from him as fear brought with it sobriety.

The man with the speech impediment moved close to Clarence, "Now you would not be lying to us would you young Clawence? Because my friend Benjamin here does not like people lying to him. Do you Benny?"

The hot stinking breath of the second assailant cursed Clarence's nostrils, "Nah we don't Mr. Chinigan."

"I promise you I don't know where she is. I am also looking for her." The words tumbled from his quivering lips as he trembled at the urinal.

"Vewy well Clawence. But I would very much

like it if you were to stop your search as my… employer, wishes to have her to himself." Both men backed away. "Please finish your business and don't forget to wash your hands eh." The second man wiped his blade on Clarence's shoulder and laughed.

Clarence stood at the trough and burst into tears as the two men left. A second later and Ace walked in.

"What the hell happened in here buddy? You ok?"

The young man shook his head and turned to face his new friend, "I need to wash my hands."

"Did those guys hurt ya?"

"Not physically no."

"Then what's goin on here?"

"They said they would do bad things if I didn't stop looking for Kelly. They threatened me and I was so afraid Ace. I'm no man, I'm just a weak little mouse."

"Gosh darn it. You ain't no mouse, you're a man with a brave heart who ain't afraid to cry." He pulled two revolvers from his coat. "This is how we deal with their kind in the states. You with me chum?"

A tearfully, red eyed Clarence turned and looked at the alcohol crazed American, he looked at the two large shiny guns and smiled. "I'm not a mouse. I'm a man in love with a woman!" Clarence sniffed and continued, "Jolly gosh darn it. I most certainly am."

Ships in the night.

Kelly stood in her new room and looked at herself in the mirror. The dress that Madam Dreadful had given her was the perfect fit and the subtle make up almost made her look alive. She twirled and curtsied at her reflection, "Oh good morrow sir, my name is miss Kelly and I am very pleased to meet with you." She had been listening to how the other girls had spoken to the gentlemen who came to Penny's Den and was trying to mimic them, they had lots of boyfriends and that's what Kelly wanted, love and attention. "Oh no sir, I'm a lady and you must be polite."

Suddenly the door opened and Madam Dreadful slid in as if she were on ice skates. "My darling Kelly. I must speak with you."

"Miss Penny. Please." She curtsied.

"I must know something if I may pry." She sat on the edge of the bed, "Come sit with me," she said as she patted the bed.

Kelly sat and had her hands instantly grasped by Penny. "Whatever is it Madam?"

"Darling. To help you, I must know what it is that haunts you."

"I wish I could tell you but…"

"But?"

Kelly stood and walked to the window, "But…" And there, outside, running through the snow with a man in a cowboy hat was a man, "Clarence?" She shouted as she ran past the Madam and through the corridors.

The front door flew open as she ran out into the cold night, bare footed but not feeling a thing apart from something in her dead heart.

"Clarence… Clarence?" She called, rotating on the spot and shouting at the top of her voice, "Clarence!" But no one came apart from a soft hand on her shoulder.

"Darling?"

Kelly turned and stared at Madam Dreadful, "I thought… I thought I saw Clarence."

"Sometimes the heart shows us what we want to see but in reality, it is a mere illusion. Come child we must go in before you catch you're death."

Kelly stopped and stared intently into the eyes of the Madam.

"Whatever is it child."

"Miss Dreadful, I… I'm already dead!"

Penny hugged the girl and looked out at the snow and at the figure lurking in the shadows. "There there darling. I know. You are safe here." But an evil grin crept across her face as she nodded gently at the ghostly, black shape in the alleyway, it nodded back, cocked its top hat and slide back into the darkness.

"Did you hear that?" Clarence looked up at the sky as flakes of snow touched his eye lashes, "I'm sure I just heard my name."
"Hey ya don't wanna be listening to ya drunken head buddy."
"But I'm sure I heard it. It sounded just like Kelly."
Ace walked over and placed a big arm around his shoulder, "Ah shucks, I'm sorry. I've been there. Ya hear what ya wanna hear sometimes kid."
"I guess you're right Ace." He turned and began to walk back, slowly through his own foot prints.
"Where ya goin buddy? Don't ya wanna catch up with these guys? Ya know. Teach um a lesson?"
He stopped for a moment, "No. They're probably miles away by now anyway."
"Gee I guess you're right Clarence. Let's get back to that bottle eh?"
"I think I will just go to bed actually Ace. But thank you."
"Oh hey do you mind if I crash on ya floor? I kinda forgot to get a room."

The pair walked back, both following their own footprints now, but from the shadows, two pairs of eyes watched carefully like tigers with a murderous intent.

The return of Turnbuckle.

A Cockerel crowed from somewhere in the city and Kelly popped open her eyes. She had tried desperately to sleep that night, just to forget Clarence, but even if she were able to sleep like a living girl she guessed that her heart would surely not allow it. The door knocked and Kelly rolled over, "Come in." She whimpered. It was Molly.

"Ere, there's some bloke ere to see ya. He's in wiv the Madam, in 'er Boudoir."

Kelly leapt up and rushed to the door, "Perhaps its Clarence here to save me."

Molly watched the girl leave and with a smirk she whispered to herself, "I doubt it love."

The door was open and Kelly walked straight in to see Madam Dreadful sitting at the far end of the room, on her bed.

"What is it Madam? Has Clarence come for me?"

"Darling. I have something very important to discuss with you. Come to me."

Kelly's dead heart began to sink as she walked across the room, it was not going to be Clarence and the solemn look on the Madams face told a sad tale.

Suddenly the door slammed shut behind her

and as she turned, her jaw dropped.

"Hello my girl," said Maurice Turnbuckle, "I am so glad my old friend Penelope found you. It would have been an awful loss to my beloved circus if I had been unable to locate you."

Penny swept down to the side of the ring master and they embraced in a passionate kiss.

"How could you do this? You said I would be safe here. You promised me."

The pair laughed at the young girl, "You are a naïve child. I have kept you here because I was told about a special girl running loose in the city, and then, last night you told me who you were and I knew. Maurice?"

"Yes and imagine my excitement when I received the message that you had been found, safe and sound," ha said, twisting his waxed moustache.

"Please… What do you want from me?"

"Oh child have you not worked it out yet? Imagine it in lights." He waved a hand slowly through the air, "The living dead girl. She can't feel pain. She can't be killed! Try your luck if you dare."

"No!"

Turnbuckle laughed, "Oh come now Kelly, surely you of all people would have known this day would come. People will come for miles to see you, filled with a morbid curiosity and wonder at the dead girl." An evil, snarling smirk distorted his face, "Besides, all freaks should one day expect to meet with the circus."

"I'm not a freak!"

Turnbuckle walked slowly towards the girl and rubbed the back of his hand against her cheek. "Mmm so soft…" The back of his hand suddenly slammed across her face, causing her to fall to the floor in a heap and too which even Madam Dreadful let out a gasp. "Did that hurt?" He snarled.

She held her face but merely from the shock of the attack, but looking up at him she shook her head. "No," she whispered.

"And there is your answer… freak!" He extended his gloved hand, "Now come child for our carriage awaits us outside."

She snarled at him, "Never."

"Oh for goodness sake. I imagined you would resist… Strongman!" He called as the man in the leopard skin leotard appeared quickly through the door, grabbing Kelly and lifting her easily from the floor with one python-like arm.

"Goodbye darling and thank you Maurice, you were amazing last night."

Turnbuckle removed his top hat and bowed

low, "The pleasure was all mine m'lady." He kissed her gloved hand.

Kelly felt sick to the stomach as she imagined the pair of them, just over the hall from her, all night and she knew nothing about him being there. "Get your hands off of me at once you brutish man."

"Keep her quiet Strongman, I don't want anything to spoil it for me, not this time."

A large hand pressed over Kelly's mouth, muffling the screams as they moved out into the cold. "To the circus!" Shouted Turnbuckle as a heavy door slammed, encasing Kelly in the back of the carriage like a prisoner.

The place bustled with happy, busy people, packing the tents and stalls away, ready to move to the next place and ready to entertain a new town. But Kelly sat in a large caravan, alone with barred windows and a locked door. All around her were old bottles and the place smelled stale and old as if it had not been used for some time. She walked over and tried the door again, it was still locked like it had been when she had tried it five minutes ago and she knew it was futile but her desperation pushed her. Where could they be taking her? And how would Clarence ever know where she was now.

She had no idea how close he had been last night or that he had actually been just outside in the snow with the American. She noticed a dressing table at the far end of the caravan and walked slowly over to it. There were grease paints and wigs on stands, they looked old, used and dusty. As Kelly sat and stared at her reflection in the mirror she spotted a tiny purple mark on her cheek from where the ring master had hit her. She rubbed it with her finger tips and felt a small swollen area. Odd she thought, she had never had a bruise before because her blood simply did not move to cause one. But perhaps? No, it couldn't be, not that.

A Clowns belch!

 Clarence sat bolt upright and Ace fell from his chair as a drunken Clown burst through the door. "Claudia!" Shouted the fool.

 "Clarence…" Moaned Clarence as he rubbed his aching head.

 "Yes. The girl. You know the dead one?"

 The young man sat on the edge of his bed and looked up through a blur of hangover and sleep deprivation at the slurring, painted man and scratched his head. "What on earth are you talking about? Why are you here? And how did you… Oh never mind."

 The Clown grabbed an empty bottle from the side and sniffed it, "Hmm. Yes. The cards said you were here but guess what…?" He looked at the glass of whiskey on the night stand, "… May I?"

 "Why not. Be my guest," said Ace, frowning at the Clown, then at Clarence before rubbing his forehead with his palm, "I ain't gonna touch another drink ever again."

 The Clown continued, "It's like this. Your girl is down the road. In the night time lady house."

 Clarence stood sharply, forgetting his hangover in an instant. "What? We past there just last night."

Ace smiled, "Well you best go get her then buddy. Besides, I got me an airship to fly so…"
Clarence turned and shook the Americans hand wildly, "Thank you so much Ace."
"Hey. Ya never know, maybe our paths will cross again eh?" He pulled on Clarence's arm and hugged him tightly. "Til next time eh?"

The door of Penny's Den flew open and Clarence burst in, leaving his colourful Clown friend outside to get some fresh air. "Where is she?" He shouted excitedly.
"Cor blimey, ang on love. Ya looking for someone special?" Said Molly with a seductive wink.
"Kelly. Where is she?"
Molly backed up, her face suddenly grey with panic as she turned and ran up the stairs. A moment passed and the tall figure swept down the stairs in her ghost-like way. "Darling. You must be Clarence?"
Clarence by now was like an excited puppy and almost finding it impossible not to grin from ear to ear. "Yes. Is she here?"
"I am sorry sweet Clarence. But she was here."
"She spoke of me?"
"Yes but… I fear it was in a past tense. She has another and they left together just this

morning.

At that moment Clarence felt his heart rip in two and shatter like fine china. "But… But she said… I thought."

"You poor heartbroken boy. She was in tears when she spoke of you."

"She was?" Clarence felt the sorrow vanish in an instant as a cloud of distrust fogged up behind his eyes.

"Yes darling. She sobbed like a child."

Something now prickled up his neck like a moment of realisation. "I bet she had been drinking when she spoke of me. She always was emotional when she had got to drinking."

Penny placed a hand on his shoulder and looked thoughtful at him, "She had almost half of a bottle and her heart spilled out to me. But her love is with another. I am very sorry."

Clarence had never hit anyone, let alone a woman but right at that moment he wanted to strangle Penny with his bare hands. Why was she lying about Kelly? His dead girl could not cry or drink, so who had taken her and… then it hit him. He ran from the house, out to the Clown who was doing his very best to seduce a group of very uninterested looking girls.

"Clown. I need to know something. Why are you not at the Circus?"

"Oh. Yes. They said they had to let me go because I spoke to you about things that a Clown aught not be talking to you about Celina."

"Meaning?"

"I told you about your dead girl, and besides I don't travel well. I get a bit, well, ya know, vomity."

Clarence frowned, "Travel?"

"Yep, they leave today. Weren't supposed to but the ring master insisted they had other commitments or something or whatever he said before."

"But they can't. We will never get to her in time."

"We can make it."

"How? It's on the other side of the city for goodness sake."

"Taxi?" Said the Clown almost knowingly.

Clarence smiled, "Mr. Leech."

Clown was like a strange, multicoloured homing pigeon as he ran, and even though his knowledge of the city was nonexistent he seemed to have an eerie way of knowing exactly where they were going as if he had been there before; and in no time at all and through the maze of alleyways the pair had arrived on the familiar side of the city.

"Mr. Leech," called Clarence as he spotted his old friend cleaning the taxi cab.

"Well hello there Clarence. We wondered where you had got to. Are you ok and, if you don't mind me asking," He moved his head close to the lad's ear, "Why on earth are you with that grubby looking Clown?"

Clarence laughed, "I'll explain on the way."

"On the way to where young man?"

"To the circus Mr. Leech."

Nelly excelled herself in speed like a thing possessed and Clarence, at one point, wondered how a horse so old could possibly move so fast. But in no time they were at the green. The circus folk were still packing up as Clarence ran into the field, grabbing the first person he could find. "Please sir. Where is the ring master? He has Kelly."

The man in tight, white clothing looked bemused at the lad and spoke in a very camp mixture of a French and something else accent, "Well sir, the ring master always leaves before us all to announce our arrival," he made a funny ooh noise after he spoke that made Clarence feel a little uneasy.

"So he has left?"

The man wiggled his head a little and pouted,

"Oh you. I told you he has gone, you not listen to Serge?"

"So where did they go?"

"To the coast but that is all Serge is telling." He pouted again, slapped Clarence on the shoulder and cart wheeled off.

Clarence looked round to the Clown, "Come on. You know these people right?"

"Well actually Colette, I don't really know them too well, you see they made me stay in that tent for years and well, you know, people forget a Clown." He looked thoughtfully at the ground and then looked up in shock and realisation, "Mr. Fluffles?" He wailed.

"Oh yes. Where is he?"

"He was in the strongman's carriage. He loves that mans German sausages."

"We must find them, at once."

Again Nelly excelled herself and again Clarence decided it to be an odd occurrence that any horse at all could travel at such speeds while pulling a carriage, but he had other things to think about than a high speed pony.

The coast road, as it suggested, led directly to the coast. It was a main route for smugglers and highway men and many a traveller had succumbed to its villainous inhabitants and this day was to be no different.

"Woo Nelly," called Mr. Leech as he spotted the figure in black upon a jet black steed standing in the centre of the road. "Bugger," he muttered.

"Stand and deliver sir and I shall spare your life for your gold."

Mr. Leech knocked on the wall of the carriage and called through, "Just a little stop sirs. Nothing to worry about." He jumped down and walked to the robber. "Excuse us sir but we are in rather a hurry. So if you wouldn't mind." A revolver was suddenly poked against the old mans nose.

"First mistake sir. I am no man. I am Harriet Flowers, highway woman extraordinaire."

"Well bugger me. Not the notorious Harriet Flowers who be also known as Mad Harry, scourge of the highways, plague of the roads, thorn in the arse of the king? "

The slight woman bowed, "At your service, now if I may, I have work to do, people to rob etc…Namely you sir," she said as she winked at the man.

"Please. Except this coin purse and let us pass ay? There's a good love."

There was a click as Harry cocked the hammer of her gun with her thumb, "Sir. Firstly I am not you love and secondly I am not in the habit of accepting mere purses of coin so I must decline and ask, what is in the carriage?"

Mr. Leech blocked the robber's way as she moved to the left to go around him. "I'm really not at liberty to say miss."

She moved right but again the portly chap blocked her way, "Sorry miss."

"Listen to me. If you do not let me by, then I will have to put a hole in you, and I really do not wish to waste a bullet on such a kindly faced gentleman as yourself sir."

Mr. Leech sighed, "Well av it your way then ma'am." He stepped aside and watched the women walk to the taxi. He watched her and could not help but notice the way she moved, almost cat like as if she were on the prowl for her next victim, which, in fact she was. Her gloved hand grabbed the handle and she turned it slowly, pistol poised in her hand. The door opened with a creak that seemed to fill the now silent air of the country road and to the absolute astonishment of Mr Leech; the most enormous belch roared out of the carriage, accompanied by a bazaar haze that reminded him of a heat wave except this had an odd tinge of brown to it. Its ferocity was such that Harry's hat was blown clean off of her head and her knees buckled beneath her as she lost consciousness.

The Clown popped his head out from the carriage with a thumb in the air, "Lucky that weren't you eh boss?" And then he fell out of the taxi straight on top of the highway woman.

Clarence jumped down too and pulled the Clown off of the woman. "Who is she Mr. Leech?"

"She's only bloody Harriet Flowers." Said the old man as he puffed his way back to the carriage.

"Not the world renowned Mad Harry Flowers, notorious highway woman, scourge of the highways, plague of the roads and thorn in the…?"

"Yup and we've only gone and caught her with the putrid breath of old Mr Clown there."

"So what do we do with her now? We can't just leave her here, anything could happen. She could get robbed."

Mr Leach couldn't help but smile at Clarence and his pure, good honest nature. He was prepared to help a villainous scoundrel like Harriet Flowers just because she was a fellow human being in need, and even though her incapacitation from the Clowns burp was her own doing, it was his obligation to stop any bad from happening to her. "Right you are Mr Clarence."

"I suggest we tie up the horse, Chuck it the the carriage and I'll ride this criminal back to town!?" Said the Clown as he lay there, eyes still rolling in his head.

Clarence frowned at the Clowns rather odd suggestion, "We should tie her up and take her with us to the nearest police station. But perhaps an intoxicated Clown on horseback would be a bad idea. I think he will follow on his own?"

"I reckon so Mr. Clarence. Mrs. Leech always says that a good horse will follow his master anywhere." He looked down the road just in time to see the horse bolting up a bank and into the woods. "Guess that's not a good horse then?"

"Right then," said Clarence with a very new and rather authoritarian tone, "Let's get her tied up and in the back." He kicked the Clowns' leg to wake him, "Come along chap. We need to go."

"Right you are Cuthbert."

Clarence scowled at him, but chose to say nothing.

It was dark by the time Harry woke up. "What the hell's going on? Untie me at once you…

you kidnappers you," she hissed.

Clarence smiled, "Hello, I'm…"

"Bugger off!" Said Harry.

"Sorry, but you were going to rob us after all."

"Be that as it may, you don't just kidnap people. It's not polite."

"And neither is robbery."

She slouched back and made a humph noise, "Touché."

"I'm dreadfully sorry that we had to tie you up and bring you with us, but you see… Well anything could have happened to you out there while you were unconscious."

"Well I suppose that is a gallant gesture. But I can handle myself. You've heard the stories about me surely?"

Clarence nodded, "I heard that you once took on three men in a fight and you beat them all with your bare hands?"

"Well it's all true, apart from it being seven large men and a midget, and I had a broken wrist too, my right…" She paused and smiled and gently said, "Lucky I'm left handed."

"Yes I'd say. But still, it seemed like the kindest thing to do."

"Well then thanks, I guess. So why are you in such a hurry?" She said struggling a little as the taxi tilted on two wheels.

"We are chasing a carriage that came along this road."

"Oh really?"

"Yes and if we pass a police station on the way then we will drop you there if that's ok?"

Harry thought fast. It was an occupational hazard to think on your feet as a highway person and besides, she did not enjoy prison, and this time and with her record she would surely meet the gallows. "You said a carriage? What kind?"

"Oh it was a circus one."

"Big and red?"

"Yes."

"With circus written along its side?"

"Yes that's the one. Have you seen it?"

Harry smirked, "Untie me and I'll tell you."

"This is a trick isn't it?"

"Might be."

"Swear on it."

"What?"

"You heard."

"Ok." Said Harry rather reluctantly. "You have my word as a highway person. We are a very honourable people you know." And she was right too. Highwaymen and women, or highway people as they now liked to be called due to something called 'equal rights in the work place' were genuinely good people, that's if you looked past the robbery and threatening with firearms, and of course the killing and torturing and leaving people stranded in the middle of nowhere as required. There was apparently a code that went back a hundred years where your word meant your life and if you broke your word then, well, 'they' would come for you and take you life in the dead of night and it was that simple. No one really knew who 'they' were or in actual fact whether 'they' even existed at all, but it was the code and no one wanted to test it or break with a time honoured etiquette just in case.

"Very well." Clarence said as he loosened the rope and spat on his hand. "So the carriage we seek? You say you saw it?"

Harry also spat on her palm and grabbed Clarence's hand, shaking it just the once but as firmly as any man would have done. "I did indeed. It had a very large man with a bald head and curly moustache driving it. I thought it was strange that he wore a leopard skin leotard too, especially as its snowing."

"That's the strongman that is," muttered Clown as he drifted from his haze of semi unconsciousness. "He's a big bugger isn't he?" He drawled and continued to snore.

Harry leaned forward, "So why are you following them? Money? Jewels? Gold!?"

Clarence looked sentimentally at the highway woman and whispered, "Love I think."

"Oh…Really?" She screwed her face up and looked almost pained.

Clarence nodded in his little dream world.

"Well if that's your reason then good for you. Who is she? Is she rich?"

"Her name is Kelly and she is the most beautiful girl I have ever seen, and no, she isn't rich," said the lad still in his own little rose tinted world.

"That's very lovely Clarence. She must be a very special girl."

"Oh she is."

"So how did you meet her?"

"I met her at the Morgue where I work."

Harry winked, "Oh a work based romance ey?"

"Oh goodness no. She was one of the corpses."

Harry laughed but began to feel a little sick as she realised he was not joking, "Oh my gods, you're telling the truth aren't you?"

Clarence stared at her as if nothing was wrong, "Well of course I am."

The highway woman leaned forward and placed a hand on his knee, "Forgive me for asking, but isn't there a word for that kind of thing? I mean, you know, having a dalliance with dead folk?"

Clarence looked shocked, "How could you think such a thing, she isn't that kind of dead girl…"

"I'm sorry but is there any other kind?" Interrupted the confused highway woman.

"Yes there jolly well is… She is a living dead girl."

"Uh huh?"

"I'm sorry Harry, It's difficult to explain. She was dead when she came in but then wasn't."

"Oh like a zombie?"

Well no not really, but yes, for arguments sake."

Harry smiled, "Well if she's the girl for you." She sat back in the chair, "But if I could ask." She nodded at Clown, "What's with him?"

"Oh Clown? They have his dog."

Harry chose not to ask as she looked from the window, "Right!"

A little money spinner

The circus carriage thundered along the narrow road, forbidding anything that would be unfortunate enough to meet it coming the other way. The huge horses seemed to be almost cursed as they galloped at full speed as the giant Strongman whipped at them ferociously, trying to squeeze every last inch of strength from them. The carriage tilted a little as it took the left hand path of the fork in the road with an arrow shaped signpost saying South coast. The post spun from the velocity and fell to the ground, pointing its sign up another lane.

"We are making fantastic time Kelly. I so look forward to showing my new exhibit."

Kelly scowled from her caged area in which she was locked, at the ring master, with his black eyeliner and waxed moustache, "You will pay for this you horrid man."

Turnbuckle lurched forward with a hand raised and Kelly recoiled. He laughed, "You see. I have complete power over you girl. Just as I have with my other freaks. They know I am their master and they do not question me."

Kelly looked at the paintings and photos that lined the caravan. "Are these the others?"

"Ah yes." He stood and admired them. "This is

the fat man, my first freak." He stroked his chin, "Not a freak par say but a great big fat money spinner. Then there was miss Daisy Brady the bearded lady. And then the fish boy, Gil we called him and the conjoined twins and so on. But now I have the dead girl."

"You are a horrible, cruel and greedy man Maurice Turnbuckle."

He spun round and grabbed the bars of the cage, "And you are an intolerable freak who wishes to lose her tongue?"

Kelly pushed herself into the corner and felt something move in her chest.

"Ah. Look." Turnbuckle gazed out of the window, "The lights of another town and another bunch of fools, eager to part with their hard earned money."

Small houses went by as the carriage slowed down and Kelly could see that they were in a little seaside town. "Hybrook?" She whispered as they bumped and rumbled over grass and onto another green.

The carriage ground to a halt and Turnbuckle climbed out. His face full off an eager madness as he pulled a lever and a loud hiss of steam blew from the underneath like a train. Both sides began to slowly move out, rotate and then rise into the air. Another pull of another lever and a whirring noise filled the carriage as the steam powered generator rumbled into action. "Electric." Called the ring master as the huge sign lit up with a flicker and filled the sky with the words CIRCUS. "Roll up, Roll up. The circus is coming to town," shouted Turnbuckle as he leaped from the carriage. A small gathering of people had already clustered around the man, in awe of the lights like moths to a flame, as the ring master handed out flyers. "Tell all of your friends and family and see the greatest show on earth. He raised his arms like a winner and let go of the leaflets. They blew in the air, taking the wind and raising up through the twilight like colourfully printed leaves. Several floated down into the high street, onto the pavement and into the path of Doctor Andrew as he made his way from his surgery. He picked one up and read the words out loud as he puffed on his pipe, "Turnbuckles circus. See the newest attraction first. Come and wonder at the living dead girl." He looked up, "My gods she's back in Hybrook."

Turnbuckle climbed back into the carriage and pulled a chair up in front of the cage. "In just one day. You will become a cog in the machinery of this circus. You shall have the lead role in my carnival of the macabre. What say you child?"

Kelly sat and stared at the floor.

"Are you not excited by the prospect of this? You will be a star of my making."

"But you plan to hurt me. How can I be excited about that?"

"Ha! You proved to me that you feel no pain so stop that lie at once. Your purpose in life is to make me lots of money." He drummed his fingers together and smirked, "Lots and lots of money."

What lies beneath?

Beneath the streets of Ashwood lay a maze. It had been there for as long as the city had stood and its rodent population outnumbered the humans walking above by one hundred to one. It was the sophisticated network of the Ashwoods sewer system and with its jumble of pipes and tunnels, it could be a frightful and deadly environment for anyone lost down there. But through the drip drop of water and squeaking of rats, another sound mumbled through the tunnels and echoed around corners like a haunted house. Within the centre of the sewer system and directly below the cathedral stood an ancient area, full of barrels and sarcophagi. A place that had been untainted and that was built long before the sewer system itself had been created around it. The place was now forgotten by most but riddled with ancient mystery and an ambient air of the occult. This occult air took the form of a group of white robed figures, circled around another figure in a black hooded cloak. Black candles burned in the shape of a triangle, illuminating the man in the centre as wisps' of incense smoke floated around him.

"Brothers and sisters of the seventh moon. Keepers of deaths secrets. Behold." He held up a news paper, "See here. I, the keeper of the key, bring you news. The sacred items are now ours once again, stolen back from those heretics who wish to stop our magic's. The sacred black robe from Ashwood. The staff of Mahooganooba that we recaptured from the Desert plains." He pointed at a small stone plinth that was covered with inscriptions, "And now the prophecy is upon us. The dead have risen and so we must cast forth to use the powers it bestows. Once our almighty mystic leader takes the final artifact from Romania we shall go to south America for the final days and live out the prophecy."

There was a cough and then a timid voice spoke, "Sorry oh deathly mystic leader, but, well, did the prophets not say it would be another thousand years before the rising?" Said a small man at the back of the circle as he waved a hand.

"Brother Markus. We have been blessed this moon. Our sacrifices have bought with them the ultimate gift and the three sacred items are soon to be together for the ritual." He held up the circus flyer, "See, the dead girl!"

"A circus entertainer? Really?"

"Yes but a dead circus entertainer none the less brother."

The others gasped at the piece of crumpled paper.

"And so now my friends, we shall go and see this dead girl and we shall take her in the name of the Necromancers and for the sake of our Almighty one."

A generalised, haunting chant began to echo about the tunnels again, but a hand rose from the back of the circle for a second time.

The mystic leader rolled his eyes, "What is it now Brother Marcus?"

"Well this dead girl. What if she is just, well, you know, like another one of those funny circus freaks and not actually 'the' dead one?"

"The spirits speak and they tell us that it is time."

"But?"

"Brother Marcus."

"But?"

"BROTHER MARCUS!"

"Yes?"

"Shut it!"

Cobblers what now?

Nelly's hooves clipped and clopped over the stones in the road as they entered the small village. Clarence leaned from the window, "What's happening Mr. Leech? Are we there?"

"I'm afraid not young sir. Seems Nelly threw a shoe and well… I may have taken a wrong turn a few mile back there."

"Oh," said Clarence, in a most dejected tone. "Well at least we can take a rest and besides, I think the Clown needs refuelling."

The trio jumped from the taxi and took a look around. The village was beautiful like a picturesque post card in the fine dusting of snow. A small boy ran up to the Clown and leaped up and down in front of him like an annoyingly loud spring, "Please sir. Are you the circus."

Clown blinked and looked confused at the child, "Cuthbert, what do I say? I'm not really allowed near children since… well since I set fire to the last lot I was with."

Clarence shrugged, "I'm not very good with children either." Suddenly the pair were amazed to see Harry juggling with three apples.

"Well that saved us," said Clarence.

Harry threw one apple to the boy, dropped the second into her pocket and the third in her mouth, much to the delight of the small gathering of villagers who now surrounded the group. She crouched down and ruffled the boy's hair. "We got split up from our circus. Do you know where we can find them?"

"Don't know anything about a circus miss." Boomed the voice of a very large police constable as he pushed his way to the front. Harry stood to attention and gulped but the Bobby didn't seem to recognise the criminal. "PC Brash is the name and I welcome the four of ya to Cobblers Knob."

Clarence and the Clown began to snigger like children and even straight talking Harry had to bite her lip.

"We're in Cobblers Knob?" Mr. Leech said as he bumbled through the audience. "Well then you must know my cousin Brian? He's a blacksmith and a very good taxidermist much like myself."

"Why yes. He lives at the other side of the village. Right down in Cobblers Knob End." The policeman beamed as he pointed down the lane. "Oh, but don't be going to far down the lane else you'll be in Bells End which is the next village along.

At that point the other three dissolved into tears of laughter.

"Are they alright?" Said the policeman.

"Oh I reckon it's just all the travelling is all. Now I'm just off to get Nelly re-shoed and say hello to my kin. Why don't you lot go off and explore."

The little boy grabbed Harry's hand and grinned at her, but then his eyes narrowed as he noticed the revolver in her coat. "Are you here to kill the witch?"

The villagers gasped in unison.

"Witch?" Laughed Harry, "Oh goodness no." She looked at the Policeman, "Witch?"

"Oh aye miss. In the forest there be a witch. Runs about as naked as a jay bird and…" He placed a hand to the side of his mouth, trying to conceal his words from the other villagers, "She has a dragon too."

The villages gasped again and there was much muttering about dragons and witches and nakedness.

"A dragon? Don't be preposterous, they don't…"

The Policeman interrupted, finishing the sentence for Harry, "Exist? Oh they do, seen it with me own eyes too. All green and leafy like, with it's funny mooing noise to confuse ya into

a false sense of thingy ma bobs."
 "Security?"
 "Nope, definitely a dragon."
 Harry frowned. "Well we aren't here to…"
Again she was interrupted.
 "There be a reward in it for ya. And besides, if you've got that there gun and you ain't ere to kill the witch and her dragon? Well then I'd have to confiscate it from ya and ask why ya got it on ya!?"
 Harry stared into nothing as imaginary coins dropped before her eyes like a rain of gold, and she realised she may be onto something. "Well one little look couldn't hurt could it?" She said with a mischievous look in her eye as the crowd cheered.
 Night fell upon the village of Cobblers Knob and Harry sat in the pub with Clarence and Clown. Two men sat on a raised area in the corner with guitars and one had a mouth organ that was balanced on a frame work around his neck. There was a photograph in between them of another man. They looked a little familiar to Clarence but he could not quite put his finger on where he had seen the gentlemen before. He stared for a moment at the duo and then at the guitar case in front of the stage that had large, worn out letters on it that read, C. A.

Daver. Clarence scratched his head, "Cadaver?" He whispered, but was brought back into the conversation with his friends as Harry bumped a fist onto the table.

"Look. If this witch thing is true then there could be some money in it for me…I mean us." She said as she tightened the laces of her knee length boots.

Clarence took a sip of his ale, "And what if this witch is nothing more than a myth? You know, a fairy tale like werewolves and Vampires and stuff? What are you going to do then?"

She stood up and tied her hair back into a pony tail, slipped her long coat on and placed the hat on her head, "Then I shall improvise sir." She winked and left the building.

"I so would," said as he dreamily watched the woman leave the pub.

"And she so would break your fingers." Chuckled Clarence.

The Clown hiccoughed and gulped from the bottle, "Fairly enough, Carl."

Clarence rolled his eyes, choosing not to entertain the fact that Clown had got his name wrong for the umpteenth time since they had first met and considering his psychic abilities he was really rather crap with names.

Here be witches… and a dragon?
   The moon sat, silvery and fat in the sky like a big lamp, lighting the way through the little path that led into the heart of the woods. Harry sniffed in the cold air and an underlying smell of wood burning tested her nostrils, her keen senses twitching at every sound and smell like a wolf. She wasn't the kind to get scared easy and even when faced with gangs of thieves she was able to stand her own and fight them fearlessly, but right there and then something gripped the highway woman. Perhaps it had been the hype from the villagers that was starting to work its way into her subconscious, but a trickle of fear crept up her neck with a shudder of goose bumps, there was some bad vibes in this forest thought the highway woman.
   The path was becoming narrow now and a low mooing sound came from just up ahead. Harry remembered hearing PC Brash mention that the dragon would moo like a cow to confuse its prey before it gobbled them up whole and she shuddered as she pulled the gun from her coat, just in case. Suddenly a white figure blurred across the path from one side of the woods to the other like a ghost and a cackle shrilled

through the still night air. Harry's heart thumped in her chest and she pulled the second gun from her coat, holding them both at arm's length in front of her. "Stand and deliver," she called instinctively. The figure rushed past again. "Who goes there? I'm well-armed and I will shoot you."

A ghostly voice whispered through the frozen air, "Would you shoot at an old lady?" The words seemed to come from everywhere, maybe carried on the breeze or a trick of the dense woodland, but its eeriness spooked Harry to the bones.

"If you were a witch then yes I jolly well would," she called bravely.

"Then I am not a witch and you may not shoot at me yeeees." The voice now came with a haunting screech and cackling laughter.

Harry looked through a furrowed brow. "Show yourself then and I will not shoot you."

There was a moment of silence before another eerie cackle split through the quiet air, "Make your way down the path my pretty thing and you will find my humble dwelling."

"It better not be made of bloody gingerbread!." She whispered.

The cackle disappeared off into the dark, thick blanket of the forest and Harry followed it slowly. The wind now whistled through the trees and an owl hooted as twigs grabbed at her hair like tiny wooden hands, pulling and scratching her. Then, as if walking into another world, and standing lonely in the clearing there stood a beautiful, white cottage with dark wooden beams and a quaint little thatched roof that rounded at the bottom like a muffin top. A large, fat and rather grubby looking cow stood in the front garden and looked up for a second as in munched on is cud. "Moo." It said. It was completely covered in leaves and bind weed but seemed more than content to be munching on the vines that grew around its rotund body. There were pretty flowers of all colours sprouting from all over the garden and the smell from them seemed to wisp about Harry's nostrils almost enticing her to come closer. Small birds flitted about the place too, seemingly unaware that it was the middle of the night, and the air was warm with a distinct lack of snow.

 The front door of the little house opened slowly and the voice called out, "Come, Come, yeees!" It beckoned.

 Harry walked cautiously toward the cottage, scratching a gloved finger over the door frame just to make sure it was wooden and not made out of gingerbread.

"Well? Come in then," the voice screeched.

The interior was just as quaint and pretty as the exterior with a little fire burning and cosy arm chairs and doily's. "Hello?"

From the kitchen, a little old lady appeared and as suggested by PC Brash, she was completely naked as the proverbial jay bird, with only her incredibly long, white hair to protect her modesty. "Oh my," said a startled Harry.

"Do sit down," said the naked old woman as she placed a plate of scones on the little round table, "Tea?" She screeched before scuttling back to the other room.

"Urm yes please." Not a great deal ever surprised Harry, and she had seen many a peculiar sight while on the highways, but the nakedness of the crazy little old lady startled her somewhat.

"So? They sent you to find the naked witch yeees?" Shouted the naked witch from the kitchen. "Sent you to kill me and my dragon did they?" She appeared with a tray of tea making apparatus. "Promised you riches did they?"

"Urm well yes to all of those things as it happens." Stuttered the now embarrassed highway woman as she fought with what looked like two forks welded together amongst an array of tea making instruments. Harry had obviously sat for tea before but the tray contained so many foreign instruments that she might as well be in an operating theatre, was a cup of tea supposed to be this complex?

The naked witch beamed a toothless smile and Harry couldn't help but feel pulled by the heart as she looked at her adorably wrinkled face.

"So are you a real witch like they all say?"

"Yeees!" Screeched the naked old lady.

"I've never met a real witch before," said Harry as she plopped a sugar cube into the cup with another device that resembled a spoon stuck to a fork.

"Drink! Eat!" She shouted.

Harry sipped the sweet tea and nibbled at the corner of a scone, it was all really rather delicious, especially the green bites.

"Yes, Yeees," shouted the witch with excitement.

"It is very nice thank you."

"Yes?"

"But why do the village folk dislike you so much?"

"Hmm? They think I will curse them because I am a witch and they think my cow is a dragon, yeees. Mmm. Eat it!" She ordered.

Harry obediently nibbled some more of the

scone which seemed more delicious than the previous bite. "Are you a white witch?"

The naked witch cackled, "There's no other kind child. We all do spells and make potions, but I've never seen one ride a broomstick nor eat a child," she cackled again and Harry joined her with a nervous giggle.

"These scones really are scrumptious. May I have another?"

The witch nodded frantically, "Yeees, YEEES!" Her eyes now like big green saucers and almost spinning in their sockets.

Harry felt a little, cuddly feeling wash up from the soles of her feet and into her jaw as she chewed the doughy scone, it tasted really rather nice as she felt the urge to chew harder. "So do you make your own cakes?"

"Yeees." She pointed to a large bush in the corner of the room, "It's from the Americas and it adds the right spice to um."

"It looks a little like a tomato plant," said Harry as she lazily took another scone from the tray.

"Don't taste like tomatoes though does it?"

Harry looked again at the old lady and pondered at how anyone would be afraid of such an adorable, if not a little eccentric old woman. "But there must surely be more to this story than that? I mean you are a little old lady, living on your own in the woods with a rather scruffy pet cow. What on earth possessed them to think otherwise?"

She gummed on a scone and snatched Harry's cup from her, and staring into the bottom of it. "Many years ago there was a man and he had a horse… It died!" The pause was a little uncomfortable as it lasted just that tiny bit too long. "And he asked for me to bring it back to life."

"Right? And?" Said a now very intrigued and rather mellowed Harry.

She pressed her eye against the tea cup and continued, "I did as he asked. But on the conditions of the spell, it was written that he who cheats death, must live a life in the service of death."

"What? Like the dead girl?"

The witch smiled gently and the tone in her voice changed to that of a soft, almost harmonic whisper "So the visions and voices were true? A dead girl walks among us once more?"

Harry felt a little uneasy as the witch poked a finger into the tea cup. "Yes it is true but she isn't like a normal walking dead type. Clarence says she is real like you and I apparently."

"Ah yes and the Clarence? The Clarence,

hmmmm. He means to save the dead girl yeees?"

"Quite. Yes, well I imagine so."

"There are others who wish to take the girl from the Clarence too. A great wizard shall be one. Beware for he is a sheep in a wolfs clothes yeeees."

"Do you not mean a wolf in sheep's clothing?" Questioned Harry.

The naked witch looked from the cup with a very wide left eye, "One will die!" She shouted.

"What?" Harry coughed on the remaining scone in a flurry of crumbs, "Who?"

"Not you, but one of your party. He will die for death and you… You will find love with a foreigner."

"Love? I do not think so madam." Now there was one thing that scared Harry to the core, and that was the 'L' word as she liked, or rather disliked to call it. She had been in love once before and it had ended in the most disastrous circumstances of which she never wished to remember, but as she tried to forget, all she could do was remember. He had been a bandit, on the run from goodness knows what and he had stumbled upon the small farmhouse where Harry had lived. She had only been seventeen at the time, but old enough to know that the

man before her was a bad sort, and that just compelled her more. She had fallen instantly head over heels for the scoundrel. Her mother had let the man stay, and over the months his feelings for the Harriet grew too, as did hers for the criminal. But then that one night, when the lawmen came and that large policeman had burst in with his revolver and ginger sideburns, shouting and screaming. Harry had stood behind her love, but he had grabbed her and used her to shield himself from danger. The rage and shame pulsated through her as she stood up, trying to forget the hideous memory of that night.
"I must go. I'm sorry."
"But you haven't finished your tea."
"Thank you for your hospitality but…" As she ran from the house into the night she heard the voice of the witch one last time.
"Beware the Necromancers for they watch him, Yees, watch, WATCH." She cackled and it seemed to echo out into the night and through the woods to the village like a phantom.
Harry stomped through the undergrowth, gritting her teeth and remembering why she hated men.
She sniffed and wiped an unwelcome and very uncharacteristic lone tear from her eye.

A deal in death

Clarence watched the snoring Clown in front of him and wondered how a man could get to such a low ebb. It was heart breaking to think of. A Clown was supposed to be the height of fun and happiness but there he was, looking at the irony that was Clown. "Clown?"

"Fluffles." He muttered.

"You poor sad man." He looked over to the barkeeper, "Keep an eye on him would you sir. I need a little air."

The night was bitterly cold but the sky was clear enough to see every star up there in the heavens, all of those constellations. He wondered if anyone watched from the other side of those stars as he looked out, another Clarence perhaps, or even an alternate Clarence called Clarice who was searching for a dead boy called Kevin. It was then that he began to ponder on a god and whether or not there was a heaven for all the dead that had passed through Wilkomsirs family morticians. Perhaps his little micro religion for one was just a fantasy and that there was something bigger out there in the afterworld. He wondered if Kelly had seen heaven, or any sort of heavenly place, or in fact, maybe it had not wanted her and that was why she was still here. Perhaps she had been a dreadful person before and this was the gods way of giving her some kind of second chance. Whatever it was it was causing Clarence to have one of his headaches and he thought for a moment if she was thinking about him right now? He hoped for nothing more than that, that she was looking up at the stars thinking about her Clarence Bunn and then his bottom lip began to quiver. "Pull yourself together Bunn." He mumbled to himself as he marched out into the night to find Mr. Leech.

A large house was lighting up the end of the village and Clarence guessed that it was Brian Leech's place as a sign pointing in that direction read Leech's on Knobs End. As he reached the house, he could see movement from inside a large shed to the left with voices that sounded like Mr. Leech and so he pushed his face through the gap in the door. To his horror he saw Brian stuffing straw into the side of old Nelly like a stuffed animal.

"Oh my goodness."

Both men turned with a start. "Mr. Clarence sir, what on earth are you doing here?"

"I would ask you the same Mr. Leech. Is Nelly?"

Mr. Leech's cousin Brian spoke, "Yes laddie

she's dead."

"But how?" He entered the little workshop and walked up and down, examining the now, obviously patchwork horse. "Old Nelly's a stuffed animal?"

Mr. Leech put a hand on the young man's shoulder, "Yup. Has been for years now." Nelly whinnied. "You're a good ol' girl aren't ya Nelly."

Brian continued to stuff the horse with what looked like a mixture of straw and feathers, "Is old pops fault. Silly old bugger," he mumbled as he continued stuffing.

"What does he mean Mr. Leech?"

The old man looked serious all of a sudden. "Our grandfather used to own Nelly but she died and, well, he couldn't afford to live without his old work horse so he found that old witch in the woods. Made her cast a spell on ol' Nelly here and…" He patted the horse on the neck, "…Here she is now, dead as door nails but as alive as, well, as well as dead horse could be I s'pose."

"Tell em about the condition." Coughed Brian, attempting to subtly prompt his cousin.

"Condition?" Quizzed Clarence.

"Yup. The condition was that the family pay in death else they would all die."

Clarence scratched his head, "But how would you pay in death? Do you have to kill people or something?" He backed up a little just in case.

"Oh don't be daft Mr. Clarence," chuckled Mr. Leech, "It means that we all have to work in some way with the dead, help him out like. Some of us have been Morticians like your good self and some have worked in the funeral business but we found that a hobby in taxidermy had just the same effect and…" Brian huffed in the background as he started sewing the horse back together again. "…That's what we all do these days."

Clarence shuddered at the thought as he watched Brian nibble through the thick, blue taxidermal suture. "But you will all die if you chose not to work with the dead?"

"That's right. A painful and horrible death apparently," smiled Mr. Leech in such a jovial manner that he may as well be talking about the weather. "Thanks Brian. I'll be back in the morning for Nelly."

Brian grumbled something about his wife and pubs and wandered of thorough a door.

"Let's go get some rest ay boy."

As the men walked down the lane they saw a figure running towards them. "Harry?" Said Clarence.

"Clarence. The witch said that she knows about you and someone…one of us will die and I'll find love and… Necromancers?"

Mr. Leech gasped. "What did she say there about Necromancers Harry?"

"She said they watch him." Her finger pointed at Clarence, "And I can only imagine they mean you."

"Me? But?" He looked at Mr. Leech. "Who are the Necromancers?"

"They're sorcerers. Deal in death and the spirits. Nasty bits of work if ya ask me." He looked up at the moon. "Oh bugger."

"What?" Said Clarence.

"Be a full moon coming and that's when they come out. We best leave first thing."

A Cockerel crowed in the street and Clarence wandered, bleary eyed from the tavern. Mr. Leach was already outside, readying Nelly and the carriage and talking to Brian. "You need to follow the road back south and then stick to the coast road, is the only way you will find that circus. And don't be caught in the dark on a full moon ya hear?"

"Thanks Brian." Mr Leech was fully aware of why he shouldn't be in the countryside at night when the moon was full but that was the least of his worries at that moment. He was more concerned about the menacing evil that was the Necromancers and he couldn't shake off the thought of one of his friends dying. Clarence noticed how stern Mr. Leech still looked and it unnerved him a little. Mr. Leech was never the type to worry, he was the type to tell you it would all be fine in the morning and then tell you one of Mrs. Leech's sayings, but not today. Today a black cloud hung over the old man and it worried Clarence to see his old friend with such heavy thoughts.

The trio jumped into the carriage and Mr. Leech climbed up to the driving seat, still looking stern and saying nothing.

"Yaah!" He shouted and Nelly was off.

You can't kill a dead girl

Music played and the people gathered to see the entertainers on stilts and the acrobats balancing on one another's shoulders. The tents buzzed with families, excited to see the tiny woman and the man in the box. They cued to see the fish boy and the bearded lady as the Strongman lifted large groups of squealing children and spun them like a carousel. They cautiously pondered over the mans head in a jar and the turtle family while others watched the lion tamer whip the big cats from behind the safety of a chair.

But deep within the dark and sinister areas of the circus the Ring Master had an audience of his very own. "Tonight will be your night Dead girl. Tonight I shall make you a star." Turnbuckle smiled at Kelly. "And you will make me rich, do you understand?"

"Please don't do this," whimpered Kelly as she struggled to get free of the leather straps that held her firm against the upturned table.

"Too late." He grinned and burst forward through the curtain, "Roll up. Roll up and see the very spawn from hell. She is the Dead Girl and for a price you can see how she feels no pain. Stab her. Burn her. Try to kill her." He looked round and grinned at the terrified girl. "She does not break or bleed. Is she a doll of the devil or a cursed demon?"

The curtain moved back to reveal Kelly, centre stage before the baying crowd of privileged guests.

"See here one and all." The ring master pulled a rapier sword from his side and, turning swiftly he thrust it through the girl's chest. A gasp went up from the astonished audience. "See. No blood and no screams. She is a true freak of nature. A whore of Satan himself."

Kelly looked round at the people, they stared at her and then a man stood up. He climbed up onto the stage and walked to the girl. She looked at him, into his eyes.
"Please don't do this."

"You have no soul. Your eyes are dead as a corpse," he hissed as he struck a match and placed it under Kelly's chin with his hand holding her forehead. "My gods you are a freak." He turned and addressed the room, "It's true. She does not even burn. She's the devil!" He threw a bag of coins to Turnbuckle and walked back to his excitable companions with his arms raised, almost triumphantly.

That night, many came, paying great sums of money to Turnbuckle for a chance at hurting the Dead Girl and that night for the first time Kelly cried. She sobbed uncontrollably but no tears came, just the shear mental and emotion agony of what had happened to her in that tent. Men, woman and even children had poked, stabbed, burned and hit the girl, all with the morbid intent to cause her pain. She stared out at the moon and cried for Clarence. Was this what she had become? A freak to entertain them in Turnbuckles macabre show?

"Dead Girl?"

Kelly turned and saw a man peering in through a little barred window. "Are you here to try and hurt me for free?" She whimpered.

The dark figure pressed his bearded face against the bars, "Nope. I sees ya there at the shoreline. I sees ya dead and now ya not." He mumbled a little. "It not be right. I found ya, an they took ya away for this?"

"Who are you?"

He disappeared for a moment and the sound of keys jangling could be heard and then the door suddenly opened.

Kelly stood and grabbed the bars of the cage as the man wandered in and fiddled for a moment with the lock, there was a click and the door opened. She lurched forward and hugged the man, almost collapsing at his feet. She noticed a strong smell of fish but she didn't care, he had just saved her from a fate worse than life.

"They calls me the Gull man."

"Well thank you Gull man. You have saved me. But how did you open the doors?"

"All sorts gets washed up on my beach…" He raised a bundle of odd shaped keys as he smiled a gummy grin, "Including skeleton keys." He jangled the peculiar looking keys again, some were metal, others were made of bone. He helped Kelly down the steps, "We don't have much time. We best be off before they gets wind of yer escaping."

Kelly nodded silently and the pair made their way through the quite, sleepy circus, between tents that stood eerily silent like multicoloured, canvas tombstones. Through the town they silently crept until they reached the sea and the little shed nestled in the cliff face that was home to the old man.

As imagined, the entire roof and garden area was covered in Sea Gulls of various sizes. Some slept while others bubbed and squawked at each other, some even fought for no apparent reason.

"Is this where you live?" Asked Kelly as she brushed her fingers against a wind chime made of shells.

"Yar. Is me fishin' shed but you can stay for a while so ya can be safe child."

The shed was like a small house with a table in the middle with pots and pans scattered about the place. A few gulls sat inside the building and one slept in a specially made nest in a huge sauce pan on the table.

"That's flash. He's a messenger gull he is."

Kelly giggled at the thought. "Well I have never heard of such a thing before."

"Ah but that's what he is. He's a quicken too. Is why we calls him flash."

Kelly sat on a chair and a gull walked to her, eyeing her with its little beady yellow eyes.

"She remembers ya. Look," said the old man.

Kelly looked down and saw something in the birds manner, something she had not seen in a sea gull before, something almost domesticated. She lowered her hand but the bird nipped at her fingers.

"She'll bite ya though," laughed the Gull man a little to late.

"Thank you for the warning," giggled the girl.

"So ya got a message then?"

"Yes but how?"

"Write it on thar an flash'll take it to…" He paused, pushed an old piece of paper to Kelly and puffed on his pipe as he mused at the ceiling for a moment…"To where ya want it a go?"

"It must go straight to Clarence. But I don't know where he would be."

Gull man nodded and looked thoughtful, "Gulls know ya know? Got a sixth sense for finding' folk an that. They be mystical creatures ya see. Like ghosts an' all thems wolf men an' the likes…" He sat in front of Kelly and held out an old looking necklace from his grubby hand. From it dangled a little wooden bird, painted white and worn by the years much like its owner. "…This belonged to me father. He had it with him when he went out fishing." A sadness filled the old mans eyes as he spoke tearfully, "He had it when he was lost at see. So I asked the gulls to go find him. And they flew and they flew and they brought me this back. I tried again but they couldn't find him."

"Really? Oh that's a very sad story." She had never heard such a thing but her desperation led her to believe anything the strange old man had to say. There was something honest in his wrinkled and weathered face that made her trust him.

"Yup. But I got this so I still have a bit of my ol' dad with me. Now write ya message and we can get ol' Flash there sky bound."

Kelly took the piece of paper and looked at its yellow, dog eared corners, and then taking a half shaved down pencil she started to write. It was simple and to the point and was only four words, but that was enough.

Gull man folded the letter and then tied it around the bird's leg, then picked him up, "Now you whisper to em where ya want em to go."

"But I don't know where to send him," said Kelly desperately.

Gull man nodded, "You tell him. Tell him where he should go."

Kelly took a deep breath and leaned into the gull, "Go to Clarence. Fly to him."

The gull tilted its head, Bub, bub, bub," it said.

"He knows ya know."

"I hope so."

"And I knows so," he said with a knowing kindness from within. And then he walked outside with the bird in his hands. The rest of the birds were now awake and they stood, bumbling and looking at the old man. He held the bird at arm's length and freed him into the night, like a ghost against the black. The other birds began to screech out and for miles around the sound of other gulls rang out into the night like a haunting chorus.

Gull man nodded at Kelly, "It be done."
As the man wandered back in, Kelly continued to watch from the door way as the bird flew, circling higher and higher for a moment before it disappeared into the distance. She wondered if it would really find Clarence at all and whether perhaps the Gull man was just a crazy old man with no friends but the birds. She shut her eyes as a sharp twinge poked at her abdomen. "Pain?"

An interval in Necromancy

"Any luck?" Said the Robed man as he drummed his fingers together.

"Yes Almighty One. It would seem that the girl is in a town called Hybrook. Wiv the circus."

"Good, good. And what of the boy?"

"Oh young Clawence will not be a bother your gweatness. After Benny threatened him." He smirked like the jagged scar across his face.

"You have aided the cause greatly Mr. Chinigan and Mr. Boil."

"Fank you sir. But I must ask a question if I may?. What will you have us do now? It is just that, well Mr. Boil and myself would very much like to kill someone and, well you did say we could."

"Very well Mr. Chinigan. Never let it be said that the Necromancers do not meet their word."

"Yes sir, fank you sir."

"Find the girl and bring her to me."

"But the killing sir?"

The Almighty One sat back in his chair, "If anyone gets in your way. Kill them."

A little hubbub at the circus

The screams could be heard over the whole fairground. Turnbuckle had already smashed up his own caravan and now he was turning his fury at the strongman as he attacked him with a riding crop, "How could you let her escape? How could you do this? You have ruined me you idiot."

The giant stood and tried to think of an answer but his idle thoughts brought up a mere shrug of his shoulders.

Turnbuckle looked around at the rest of the entertainers and pointed the crop at them, "Well? Do any of you buffoons have an answer for this, this mute?"

"You av lost ere again no?" Came a voice from behind the ring master.

"La Douche? You have stolen her from me you scoundrel."

"Oh monsieur. Such rage directed at those who no nothing." Two men stood by his side. Dr Andrew and PC Brash.

"Give her back," he hissed at the grinning Frenchman.

"But I av not got the girl. It would seem I have been too late to steal her back for myself." He crouched down and picked up a white feather,

"Perhaps a bird as taken her, or she has grown wings no?"

Turnbuckle twiddled his moustache. "Don't mock me!" He paced for a moment, "It is fine. I shall find her first. She can't be far away."

"This is true monsieur." He handed the feather to the policeman and walked up to his adversary, "But I av the law and science on my side. What do you av."

Turnbuckle sneered, "I have dirty tricks and cunning. And a psychic…" But he suddenly realised that his clown was now no longer part of the circus, "Bugger!!!" He shouted through gritted teeth.

"Then we shall see eh?"

"Indeed." Snarled the ring master as he turned and addressed his staff, "Ladies and gentlemen of the circus. We are having an interval to find our lost dead girl." He turned and faced the Frenchman, "You know what to do people." There was a sudden commotion as the entire circus began to move out in all directions like a small military campaign. "I have numbers La Douche."

"And so do I my circus friend." He gestured behind him as the group of heavy set policemen with Billy clubs in hand appeared.

Turnbuckle clapped slowly, "Bravo sir. So shall

we commence this little game?"
 "Oui. Let the best man win eh?"
 Turnbuckle snarled as he turned. "Oh I intend too."

A bird in the hand is wearing socks

Nelly galloped with fire in her hooves through the tiny lanes, but without knowledge of where to go, the journey would take too long. As Mr. Leech concentrated on the road he could not help but notice something from the corner of his eye, it flicked and flashed from side to side and then above. "Shoo ya pesky bird will ya." But the gull continued with its task. It swooped at one point and hovered just over Nellie's head. "Woo Nelly." Called Mr. Leech as the bird darted up into the air and then rolled back down, where it landed on the back of the horse.

"What is it?" Clarence called as he popped his head from the carriage.

"Just this here bird sir. Been pestering us for a couple of mile now look."

Clarence walked round and looked at the large white bird. "What's that around its leg?"

"Looks like a sock to me Claire," said Clown.

"Claire?" Said Clarence in total bewilderment,"Really?"

"Yeah a sock," concluded the Clown.

Clarence shook his head, "Did you ever see a Sea Gull with socks on? In fact any bird with socks? I mean really Clown? Any animal at all to that matter."

The Clown pointed at the big white bird and said, "Yup!"

Clarence shook his head, "Well It looks like one of those tags. You know. The type you get on protected birds and racing pigeons."

"He's gonna need protecting if he tries putting me off me driving again," muttered Mr Leech. "Bloody dangerous if you ask me." He grumbled and eyed the creature with contempt.

"No I think it's one of those carrier birds," said Clarence.

"Like a pigeon?" Slurred Clown as he examined the label of his brandy bottle.

"Yes. But I have never seen a carrier Sea Gull before."

"I am actually akin with the animals. Much like that doctor Doo.. Doo… Doohicky thingy, you know? The chap in the papers?" Clown said as he leaned confidently into the bird, "See?" But the gull pecked ferociously at his hand, "Sod ya then. Bloody Mr. flappy trousers, and you can keep ya socks too."

Mr. Leech jumped down and walked slowly to the gull, "Now ya see there's an art to this Mr. Clown sir. You have to be very gentle and approach it as a friend." He held out a hand, "Hello there my little fella. Who's a pretty boy then? See, he likes me." The bird flapped its wings and squawked at the old man, nipping at his finger too, "Agh ya bugger," said the old man, "I'll stuff ya when yer dead I will." He walked away nursing his pecked digits.

"I suggest we blow its head clean off. Move aside." Harry held her revolver out and cocked the hammer, "It would save all this silly, girly behaviour."

Clarence put a hand on to her arm, lowering the weapon. "It's staring at me." And he was right too, the bird seemed to be intently watching him with its beady yellow eyes.

"Well you give it a try then Christopher," said Clown as he placed an arm round Harry's shoulder. The pair stood expectantly waiting for Clarence to meet the same fate as them while Mr Leech glared at it from a distance.

Clarence leaned over and the gull jumped onto his wrist and padded its way up to his shoulder. "Ha-ha. How's about that? I think he likes me."

"Bub, bub, bub," said the gull as it pecked at the multi coloured leg band. Clarence reached up to his shoulder and untied the little bow, releasing the paper. He unravelled it, read the words and then passed out.

"Give him a bloody drink. That'll wake him up,"

said Clown.

"Slap him and tell him to man up," barked Harry.

"What did the note say? Must've been an omen. Reckons we be doomed. Is he dead?" Bumbled Mr. Leech.

"Bub, bub, bub," said the gull as it landed on the unconscious boys chest, and pecked at his buttons of his waistcoat.

"It was from Kelly." Everyone gasped as Clarence staggered to his feet. He looked down at the crumpled piece of paper in his still clenched hand again and read it to his friends, "CLARENCE. HELP ME! It says and is signed, Kelly."

Clown scratched his wig, "But how do we know where she is Colin?"

Clarence turned the paper over and revealed the postcard picture on the other side and the big words across it. "Hybrook!"

"Clever girl." Mr. Leech beamed with joy. "Well let's waste no more time."

Clarence opened the carriage door, "We're off to the seaside chaps." He looked at the gull who was now pecking bugs from Nelly's back, "Can you take us there?" It looked at the young man and tilted its head and then with an almighty flap of its wings took to the air.

Clarence pointed to the sky, "Follow that bird."

The choice is yours
The tide was out and along the shore was a wealth of debris. The Gull man wandered ahead, poking boxes and barrels with a large stick to see if they were worth anything. Several sea gulls hovered over him and one sat on his head, balancing itself as the man moved, preferring the man's head as an outpost to the beach. Kelly watched the old hermit as he rummaged. It must have been a simple and peaceful life for him, wandering the shore line for treasures that others had disposed of or lost tragically to a violent storm. She wished it were her out there, living free of the ties and constraints of her death. The gull man suddenly started whooping and shouting and the birds around him began to screech.

"What have you found?" Kelly walked slowly down across the pebbles to the man.

The old man raised a bottle in the air. It had an unknown liquid inside but he rejoiced. "What ya reckon it be?"

Kelly smiled at the simplicity of the man's pleasure, "Shall we go and find out."

Gull man suddenly froze and pointed to the sea wall, "Who be that?"

"La Douche?" And there from the other end of

the wall she saw more figures, "Turnbuckle?"

"We'll be fine. Attaaack!" Gull man ran forward towards Turnbuckle. "I'll have ya gizzards," he shouted as he puffed his way slowly across the pebbles.

The ring master looked down at the man with a pitiful expression and swiped him across the face with the back of his gloved hand, rendering him unconscious. "Foolish little man." He wiped the glove with a handkerchief and stepped over the motionless old man, "Kelly. Darling. Come to me." He walked down the beach towards the frightened girl with his arms held out, "Perhaps I was a little rough with you before. I can change."

"Mademoiselle," called La Douche as he approached from the left. "Do not listen to this buffoon. Come now, I shall not harm you as this man has."

Now both man flanked the girl. Turnbuckle had a twinkle in his eye but a hatred in his heart that could almost be seen radiating from him like an angry heat wave of evil. She looked at La Douche. He looked sincere and was backed by several, rather cross looking policemen and a rather dashing gentleman with a doctor's bag. She looked back at the ring master and his sly eyes. Kelly knew then, that she must make a choice. Whichever man she went to had a plan, she knew Turnbuckles, but what would happen if she went with the Frenchman? Kelly bowed her head and walked to La Douche. Several officers moved forward as Turnbuckle lurched toward the girl. She turned to look as the entertainer was grabbed and restrained, his gloved hands snatching at thin air like a monster's talons, in the vain hope that he would grab her.

 La Douche placed his cloak around her shoulders and held her close. "My child, you must be so frightened, but you are safe with me now. I promise I will not harm you."

 But by now Kelly was numb to everything. Her mind was a blur of emotions and even the thought of Clarence was a deep and forgotten memory. Whatever had she got herself into now? It surely had to be better than the ridicule and shame of the circus. Peering back, one last time she caught a glimpse of the Gull man. He stood in the distance like a shadow, sea gulls flocking around him, circling and whirling like a living tornado of noise and white feather.. He raised a hand and waved as the gulls obscured him from sight and then, he was gone like a ghost.

"I remember just a few days ago. We were in this same carriage." La Douche bumped the door with his elbow, "It is fixed now though," he laughed, "And we av policemen all over it like little blue gargoyles," he chuckled.

"So this is it then? You're going to chop me up?"

La Douche looked shocked, "Mademoiselle! I wish to study you just as a botanist would study a beautiful new flower." He smiled and groomed his little beard, "If only things had been different eh? I wish I had let you know my intentions and explained."

"But I thought. Clarence said."

He took Kelly's hand and stoked her knuckles with his thumb, "It is a lack of understanding that leads us to say things we do not mean. Your Clarence does not know me from a man in street and I fear he only hears bad things from his Monsieur Wilkomsir. I am just a humble scientist and he is a jealous Mortician. I believe he wishes for my vast fortune no? Sadly, so many people cast assumptions through hearsay." He shook his head and glanced out of the window.

Kelly looked at the floor, "But when you took me. It was all so violent."

"And for this, but we did not know what to

expect. Perhaps we might have found a zombie and this is why I needed my henchmen. You can never be too sure," he laughed and sat back, "But you are no zombie. I can see this now."

"There is so much that you do not know about me Mr. La Douche and things that you should never know."

"My child, it is these very things that I must know. It is my job as an anthropologist and please, call me François, all of my friends do."

The airfield was vast and filled with the most magnificent variety of flying machines. Aeroplanes sat on the ground and loaded from great tunnels, leading from the terminal that spread its arms out like a great octopus, as balloons and airships hovered gently; floating in the sky like beautiful, multicoloured clouds. Kelly looked up in awe as a massive red and white balloon floated overhead, its giant propellers making a chomp, chomp, chomp sound as they pushed it through the sky, momentarily obscuring the sun like an eclipse. She placed her hand over her eyes to shield them from the glare and could just make out the people inside, looking through the circular windows as they waved to the people below.

Kelly waved back.

The carriage stopped and Le Douche opened the door, "My airship is just over there. Come now." He said, holding out his hand.

Kelly took it and the pair walked across the chilly field towards the most magnificent craft she had ever seen. The balloon itself was a beautiful deep purple with an immense but intricate, silver coloured structure covering it like an exoskeleton of patterned metal. The base looked more like a small house with wings that held a biplane at their tips.

"She has the planes for extra control. Just in case there is a storm. My pilots are the best in France." He winked.

"Wow." Was all Kelly could say as she marvelled at the airship, its beauty would've her breath away if she had had any to breathe.

"This will be our home until we reach my laboratory in Paris."

"France?"

La Douche chuckled, "Oui, of course. There is no other. Home sweet home as they say. You did not think we would stay here did you?"

Kelly shrugged, "Well I've never been to France before."

"Ah you will love Paris. It is the capital of romance and culture. I will show you the sights when we get there."

"I'd like that very much François." But deep inside Kelly wished it were Clarence taking her to such a magical and romantic place.

The interior of the airship was as splendid as its exterior, if not more elegant in some ways. It looked like one of those fabulous ocean liners that travelled the seas and it even had staff dressed like sailors. "Bonjour," said one man as Kelly entered, making her giggle as she curtsied and repeating the greeting, "Bonjour," she said back.

"This will be you room Kelly. Please feel free to change."

She gazed around the room and at the massive four-poster bed that sat to the right and at the most perfect dress lying across the bed. She picked it up and held it up to herself. It was so soft and as light as air.

"The finest Chinese silk."

"It's beautiful."

"Like you my child. Now please, make yourself at home. We shall be leaving very soon. Oh and there is hot running water from the steam boilers too should you wish to refresh." He bowed and backed out of the door.

Kelly sat at the large dressing table, the scents of so many bottles of exotic perfumes' caressed her nostrils and filled her mind with thoughts of spices and mysterious foreign lands. But then her thoughts went back to Clarence again. He would find this all very unusual and would probably want to be back in his little room behind the fridges at the mortuary, and she would give anything right now to be there with him. She looked at her pale face in the mirror, the lights around it making her appear whiter than usual and the dark eyeliner from Penny's den that was still there made her look more sickly than dead. There was a light rumble as the airships engines started up and Kelly could feel a bumping sensation as it began to rise gently into the air. She quickly stood and ran to the window as the ground below her began to get further away. The massive shadow of the airship cast down over the people milling around on the airfield and from that height, she could appreciate the sheer size of the airport. Planes took off and landed between the huge and various shapes of the other airships and balloons, and now as she rose higher, the landscape could be seen in its entirety like a map. Villages, towns and in the distance, cities, turned from mighty sculptures to tiny patches of colour against the green of England. Kelly wondered if Clarence could see the airship in

the sky from wherever he was and she pressed her hand against the glass, hoping that somewhere down there, he knew she was thinking about him. But now, out over the sea Kelly could see giant, eight funnelled ships that chugged coal smoke and steam into the sky, leaving trails of foam and sea birds as they went on their way. They looked like toy boats on a huge pond with great sea mammals swimming beneath like coy carp and in the very distant horizon she could see other land masses, other countries with other girls with their own stories to tell. Some could even be sadder than the one she told, the one she was living, and as she looked out across the sky at her England growing smaller in the distance, she felt the sharpness, stabbing her again in the chest. She winced and closed her eyes tight as a French voice spoke from the acoustic system that was made up of thousands of feet of copper piping that networked throughout the airship.
She placed her hand over the area that hurt and felt something move deep within, a twinge of pain perhaps, or something more sinister.

A fast exit
Clarence leaped from the carriage and stomped across the green towards the big top, closely followed by his three companions. "Where the bloody hell is she Turnbuckle?" He shouted as he saw the ring master.

"Ah Clarence, so good to see you at last. But you will not find the Dead Girl here."

There was a click as Harry raised her revolver.

"Ooh the highway woman, the one known as the bane of the police? How very amusing, and a fat taxi driver." He pointed at Clown. "And you. How are you old friend?"

Clown pushed past, "Where's Mr. Fluffles? You..." He staggered with a finger waving, drunkenly at the ring master and he said, "You bugger."

"Oh the mutt? You can have it back." He whistled and a small Jack Russell ran from behind a caravan, leaping into the Clowns arms and knocking him over. "See. I am not really that bad a man am I?" But behind his eyes it told a different story, one of cruelty and greed that showed through like a nasty stain.

Clarence furrowed his brow, "But you kidnapped Kelly and I have come to save her."

"Such a brave little man. It is a shame though, that she is probably miles away by now?"

"What do you mean by that you, you brute?"

Turnbuckle laughed, "Oh a brute is it. Such words Clarence Bunn, such words. No she was taken by the Frenchman La Douche, in his airship."

"La Douche has her?" Clarence felt himself deflate inside like some had let out all of the positive feelings from him all at once.

Turnbuckle rolled his eyes, "Is that not what I have just said?" He looked around at the growing group of circus folk and laughed, "She is probably undergoing surgery as we speak so I would forget about her if I were you."

"But you are not me sir." Clarence waved a fist at his enemy, "We must get to the airport at once."

Mr Leech saluted, "I know exactly how to get there, and fast too Mr. Clarence."

Harry nodded and slipped the gun back into her coat, "Well I've come this far so I guess it would break the code not to follow it through to the end."

Clown rolled on the floor with his dog, "You can count on me and Mr. Fluffles Conrad."

Clarence turned back to Turnbuckle. "See. Hope and friendship will see us through."

The ring master shrugged, "I'll beat you to it." And he ran to the big top. The four stood and watched as the massive tent began to fold and fall to reveal a huge balloon. It was coloured in the same red and white stripes of the big top and with propellers that were powered by several acrobats on bicycles. It rose up into the air and there on the deck stood Turnbuckle, "So long suckers," he shouted as he waved his hat at them.

Meanwhile in France

Kelly felt the pinch as the needle entered her skin, but the pain kept its distance, hiding way down deep somewhere in the girl, waiting for something to change in her body so that it could finally exist.

"Did that hurt?" Doctor Andrew looked concerned as he placed the metal syringe into the stainless steel kidney dish.

Kelly rubbed the area, perhaps through some instinctive reaction but she shook her head. "No it's fine, it didn't hurt, thank you."

Doctor Andrew smiled at the girl, "I'm glad. Maybe we can finally get to the bottom of what makes you tick eh?"

"Yes. Maybe," she whispered, but deep down she knew what that would find, just death and nothing more, she also knew they would never know her true story.

He sat opposite and looked into her eyes. He noticed the emptiness and remembered, "I saw that same look when I first met you on the beach you know. That look of sadness. That empty, soulless stare of death." He stuck a piece of cotton wool onto the incision site out of habit but continued to stare into Kelly's eyes.

"Soulless?" Asked the dead girl? "Is that what I am? Is that what people see when they look at me?"

The doctor blushed a little, "Well perhaps another word would've been better suited but yes. It is like looking upon the dead."

Kelly smiled, "Well I am dead." Her eyes made contact with Andrews and she reached for his hand, "Please help me find Clarence."

He felt the cold of her skin, unusual in its texture he thought and unlike the many other corpses that he had touched in his time as a doctor. There was something that felt almost living though, beneath the dead exterior, deep within the girl's skin that he had never felt before in a corpse. "Is that what you truly want? To find that boy?"

"Yes, more than anything else, I wish to see dear Clarence again." A sharpness suddenly made her grab her arm.

"What was that?" The Doctor frowned with concern.

"Nothing. I just…"

"Did you feel pain?"

"No. It was just a sensation in my arm." But in reality, it was what Kelly feared the very most. She had never felt pain before and now her worst nightmare was potentially rearing its ghastly head… What would father say?

A loud klaxon suddenly boomed out and a

French voice spoke from the huge copper horn on the wall.

"We are here." Andrew stood and looked from the window. "It's France. Look!"

Out on the airships deck, La Douche stood with his arms behind his back, his cane tapping on the wooden floor behind him. "My home land. She is beautiful no?"

Kelly placed her arm around the Frenchman's and held on. "Yes she is." And in the distance she could make out another green landscape, small farms dotted about with tiny dirt roads connecting them like veins, and in the very far distance she could make out a huge structure pointing up from the smog and into the sky. "What is that?"

"It is the Eiffel tower and my home of Paris."

As the ship neared the city, Kelly could see other airships moving like big, graceful bumble bees, pollinating passengers to and from the city, she had never seen such a thing, so many flying objects of so many colours and shapes. And there through the smog she could make out the giant green glass structure that was Paris Airport. It shone like an emerald beacon as its windows caught the sun's rays and shone them back up to the heavens through the brown mist, with mighty arms that reached up into the air, waiting to catch airships as they floated in to land. "How do we attach to those arms?"

La Douche laughed, "Ah my girl. It is all done with electrical magnets."

The tingle of static made the hairs on Kelly's arms stick up as the flying machine got closer to the huge arms. She rubbed at the Goosebumps on her forearms and shivered a little at this new sensation that she had never experienced before. The massive, copper coils clicked with blue sparks and wobbled as their heads reached out at the airship, sucking with an invisible power and with a heavy thump, the airship landed against the magnet. A row of steps moved suddenly and began to slowly glide into position as the whole ship was lowered into place by the mechanical arm.

"Ah. Paris." La Douche rubbed the girls hand and looked down at her. "Come now. I have friends for you to meet.

It's not what you know

 Mr. Leech gritted his teeth and his face beamed a deep red as the carriage screeched round a corner on two wheels, sparks flying like a steel mill. "Woo Nelly," he called as the they neared the airport.

 "Are we there Mr. Leech?" Shouted Clarence, leaning from the window.

 "Yes Mr. Bunn, but I think the place is shut to the public now."

 As the carriage rolled to a halt, the team jumped out and looked at the gateway to the airport. A lone guard stood on duty with a rifle over his shoulder.

 "Bugger," said Clarence. "What to do now?"

 There was a click, "I could take him out from here," said Harry as she aimed her gun at the man.

 "Good grief no, you can't just kill him. He's probably got a wife and family and all sorts."

 "Or a dog?" Offered Clown as tickled Mr Fluffles under the chin.

 Harry mumbled something and then placed the gun back into her coat.

 "Well me and Mr. Fluffles could show him a few tricks to distract him Cedric," suggested Clown.

 "Thank you Clown but I fear we may have to

wait until morning."

"Urm… Colin?" Said Clown with his finger pointing behind Clarence.

And as the young man turned he saw Harry had let her hair down and was unbuttoning her blouse to reveal a rather sumptuous cleavage, "Oh golly," said both men in unison.

"Well if I can't kill him," she winked and pushed her chest out, "Then I'll have to seduce him."

"Stop there!" The guard shouted as he pointed his gun at the approaching highway woman.

"Hello." She moved seductively towards the man and ran a rather suggestive finger up the barrel of the gun. "My sir, you do have a large weapon don't you."

"Get back woman."

Harry was a little taken aback by the man's response, most men would be dribbling wrecks even at this early stage. She knew she must up her game. "I've seen you so many times and decided that tonight was the night." She began to unbutton her blouse a little more, "A girl just loves a big strong guard in uniform."

He held the rifle up to her head, "But I don't like your kind ya bleedin' Trollop."

She shrugged her shoulders and then, in a blur of movement grabbed the rifle from the man's hands.

"Huh?" Said the startled man.

And with that, Harry head butted the man unconscious. "I most certainly am not a Trollop sir."

"Freeze!"

Harry raised her arms as she felt another gun, but this one was pressed against the back of her head.

"Drop the gun madam before I'm forced to shoot you."

She dropped the gun. "Does no one here want to be seduced for goodness sake?"

"Hush woman."

"Look, I just wanted to get in. I have a…"

"Save it for the police," interrupted the guard.

There was a sudden clang and a thud and Harry turned slowly to see the guard on the floor with a trembling Clarence standing over him with a large piece of wood clutched in his hands.

Harry lowered her arms and laughed, "Well well Clarence Bunn? Who'd have thought eh? You finally growing a pair of…"

"Plumbs!" Called Clown as he lifted a bottle of Plumbs cider from the unconscious guard's jacket, "Expensive stuff this, what a result."

"My thoughts entirely Mr. Clown," she chuckled.

"Mr. Bunn sir."

"Mr. Leech?" Clarence turned round to see his old friend.

"Sir. This is as far I go I'm afraid, me and Nelly here don't much like flying."

"But… I…" Clarence threw his arms around the old man. "I can't thank you enough Mr. Leech. You are a true friend."

"Clarence." He squeezed the boy's shoulders and stared into his eyes, "I want you to bring that girl back to Mrs. Leech and me ok."

"I will, I promise."

"Here," he said as he placed something into the lads hand, "Mrs. Leech said I aught give it ya."

Clarence looked into his palm and saw an antique ring. "But… I…"

"Shush boy. Take it and put it that girl's finger." His face looked so soft and friendly as he smiled at the lad. "And I'll be seeing ya soon right?"

"Oi!" Came a shout from down the road.

"More guards. We must go Clarence," said Harry as she ran to the gate.

"So long," called Mr. Leech as he jumped back onto the carriage, "Go Nelly." And with that, they were off into the night.

Clarence felt a lone tear run down his cheek as

he watched the taxi disappear, the end of one journey he thought as he looked at the spacious airfield. But now he had promised Mr. Leech that he would find Kelly and bring her back. He gritted his teeth and nodded at his two companions.

The airfield was abandoned apart from a few technicians working of huge pieces of airship and some old planes.

"Where to now Clarence?"

"I'm not entirely sure Harry." He spotted a glow at the far end of the field, "Let's go over there shall we?"

A large silver airship stood proudly next to its gantry. It bobbed a little in the air and had frost across its nose from the icy winds that blew across the field. It didn't have the normal look of an airship though as it was a great deal smaller and sleeker like one of those torpedoes the war ships had.

"Hello?" Clarence called as he walked up the steps. "Is anybody…"

"Clarence?" Came a very familiar voice.

"Ace? My word. How glad I am to see you."

The American grabbed Clarence' hand and shook it so vigorously that
Clarence thought it might come off, "What ya doin here buddy?"

"I'm still looking for Kelly. I believe she may have gone to France."

"Well hot dang, it just so happens that's where we're going."

"Really?"

"Yep. Just doin the last few jobs and then…" But suddenly he stopped mid sentence as he looked beyond Clarence, something had caught his eye and his entire capacity to talk in fact. "Who… who is that?"

"You know Clown?"

Ace pushed past and stood, staring from the gantry. "She is?"

"Harry? She's a highway woman."

Ace jumped down and removed his gloves and goggles as if in a trance like state. "The names Ace Franklin and you are?"

Harry blushed with wide eyes and held out her hand while pushing her still untied hair from her face, "Harriet," she muttered. The naked witch's words spiralled around her head but she couldn't quite believe them, or rather she didn't want to. "But everyone calls me Harry." The words and instincts in her head told her to scarper but her heart was exploding with something she had never felt before.

Ace bent a little and kissed her hand, "At your service ma'am."

Harry nearly fainted as she gazed into the Americans big hazel eyes. "Golly," she giggled. And this was what she had dreaded since the last time. She had made herself into a cold hearted woman, with a wall like exterior, impenetrable to men. But this time something was giving way. Those cold bricks around her heart were falling and they were falling for the American.

Clarence coughed, "Urm… I hate to break this up but the security guards are just over there and are heading this way and they look rather cross!"

"You there. You're under arrest." Seven guards now stood around with rifles aimed at the group.

"What on earth is going on out here?" Everyone looked up to see a most elegant gentleman walking from the airship. "Do you know who I am?" He called at the armed men.

One of the guards stood up and saluted, "Yes sir. You're that Flemington-ward chappy with all those inventions and such."

"I am LORD Flemington-ward the third and I will thank you to lower your weapons this instant."

"But," tried another guard before he was interrupted.

"Do you know how much this airship costs? And have you any idea who you are threatening? These are personal friends of mine you oaf."

Another guard held up his hand, "But they…"

"If you continue this charade then I shall have your jobs. Do you understand?"

By now the guards had all lowered their guns and were looking rather sheepishly at the ground like a group of naughty school boys.

"Now I suggest you all run along, otherwise you will find yourselves cleaning shoes and horse manure for the next couple of years."

The men disbanded almost as swiftly as they had appeared, leaving the group in peace. Clarence bowed at the gentleman, "Thank you your lordship, that was a generous thing to do."

The gentleman removed his top hat, "Please. Call me Hogbert. Any friend of young Ace here is a jolly good friend of mine. Now, do come inside."

Everything within the airship shone and sparkled with a brand new shimmer of silver and copper and the smell of newly polished leather filled the air. There were buttons and levers and dials all across the front with two chairs ready for a pilot and his mate. It wasn't like the average airship either and Clarence thought it looked a lot like a bus with passenger seats and portholes like a sailing ship.

"So you must be the famous Clarence?"

"Yes I am Clarence sir."

"Mr. Franklin has spoken a great deal about you and your… plight."

"You know about me?"

"Oh yes."

"Gosh," giggled nervously. He had heard a great deal about Hogbert Flemington-Ward the third too. The millionaire, entrepreneur and inventor among other things. He had single-handedly ballooned the world and had made underwater boats that could travel to unimaginable depths, it was said that he had even befriended a race of kipper people. "But I still must find Kelly. You see, she is in France apparently."

"Well my boy, I always say the more the merrier what."

Ace placed a hand on the boys shoulder, "You see. This here is the Slipstream, fastest airship ever built, and we're planning to see every continent in less than 80 days."

Harry sat with her chin cupped in her hands, staring dewy eyed at the big American, "Wow," she managed.

Ace winked at her and then looked back at

Clarence, "This puppy has self charging, quadruple processors that push four propellers… But she also has a vapour converting turbo underneath. Sucks the moisture right outta the air and converts into pure steam, giving her that extra little bit of oomph." He pulled the flying hat on and raised an eyebrow at Harry.

"Wow," said Harry again as she dissolved into her seat.

Hogbert took his pocket watch out and held up his hand as several clocks began to bong and clang and cuckoo, "Jolly good timing what?" He called.

Ace jumped into the pilot's seat and pulled a lever. The resulting hissing sound was deafening but Ace shouted above it, "Strap in ya'all." He turned a handle and the whistle of a motor began to whirr into a high pitched scream, "Combustors' at full pressure sir." He flicked three switches that in turn caused several lights to come on, "Main vaporiser drive belts in position."

"Jolly good Ace." Lord Hogbert pulled his goggles down over his eyes and strapped in as the airship slowly rose into the air.

"Ya ready for this sir?"

Flemington-Ward raised a hand, "To the future

old chap." He slammed his hand onto a large green button in the centre of the control panel and the whole ship lurched forward, sucking the passengers back into their seats with the most enormous G-force. Clown pulled a small pair of goggles over Mr. Fluffles eyes as his little doggy jowls flapped from the velocity. The night sky whizzed by outside as the airship shot through it like a meteorite, leaving behind it a tail of bright purple fumes and silver sparkles.

As the cabin pressure adjusted to the speed lord Flemington-Ward turned in his chair to address his passengers. "Lady and gentleman. We are now travelling at one hundred miles per hour which means YOU are all now part of a world record. The fastest airship in the world what."

A small and very polite round of applause and a dogs bark filled the cabin and Hogbert bowed his head, "Why thank you."

In no time, the ship was gliding over France and inland towards Paris. "Rather unfortunately we are unable to stop in Paris due to our lack of passports and mores to the point, a little disagreement I have with the local authorities there." Called Hogbert from the front of the ship "It makes us entering all rather illegal don't you know?" He said as the airship suddenly banked sharply to the right. "However, we shall be heading for my grandfathers château instead. It is a little way from Paris but there will be no one to check our papers."

"Grandfather?" Said Clarence curiously. "Wouldn't that make him."

"Rather old? Yes, but he really is a rather lovely old chap and very wise too if not a little on the eccentric side."

As lord Flemington-Ward continued, Clarence gazed thoughtfully from the window at the now changing scenery as it morphed into rolling hills and meadows, dusted with a white sprinkling of snow like a big patchwork Christmas cake. But before the snowy scene, he could see his own reflection looking back at him from the window like a gaunt and ghostly reminder of who he really was, because no matter how much he thought of the adventure, his mind would drag him back and remind him that he was no hero. He looked at Ace, piloting the ship, what a brave chap he was, a real hero. An American, gunslinging hero. He sighed and watched a bird flapping frantically in the slipstream next to the airship, "Silly gull." He thought as he frowned and looked back at his friends. There was Clown with his Mr. Fluffles and Harry had found love with Ace and even Hogbert, who was waffling on to anyone that cared to listen, seemed obliviously happy in his record breaking feat. He realised his life was much more like the bird outside, frantically flapping his wings in order to catch up with life, but never really getting there at the same time as all the rest of the world around him. No matter how hard he flapped his metaphorical wings, life was always several flaps ahead.

He could see a large mansion ahead and realised that it must be the château, as the ship banked again and slowed, ready to land. They were miles from Paris now and, although they had not even landed yet, Clarence wondered when they would be leaving for the city in search of Kelly.

A thud rocked the airship as it touched down on the gravel drive and the door popped open like a cork, letting out the hiss of pressurised air.

A very elderly butler stood holding a tray of Champaign in front of him, peering down his nose at the group as they exited the airship.

"Lord Effington is waiting inside sir. May I offer you a glass?"

"Thank you Pile, but I think that will be all."

"Very well sir," said the butler as he shuffled off just before Clarence could take a glass of

Champaign.

The young man was in awe at the size of the house, it seemed so much larger from the ground as it seemed to stretch out for acres either side of its giant front doors. He had never seen a house with turrets before either, and was sure that right was only reserved for castles, but this place had them lining the rooftop like a fancy castle.

"What is this place Mr, Lord, Hogbert sir? If you don't mind me asking Sir," stuttered the young lad as he caught up with the Lord.

"Oh this is just our winter retreat, nothing too fancy. It's called Effing house after my great grandfather Lord Effington-brolly. He was a wonderful man, made his fortune in diamonds don't you know, and please dear boy, it's just Hogbert."

"Well it certainly is large," he said, still gazing up in wonder as they walked through the doors into a magnificent hall. The sound of a piano playing from somewhere filled the house and echoed around the hall. "Is this the main hall?"

"Oh good lord no, this is the reception dear boy."

Clarence gulped, the space was bigger than the entire town hall back home and he could only imagine what other wonders surrounded him.

"Hogbert my boy," said a very elderly gentleman being pushed in a bath chair, "How jolly good to see you." He was being pushed by a rather muscular man in a white tunic.

"Is this the new help grandpapa?"

"Oh yes, his name is Rupert. Doesn't say much due to being a foreigner but gives a rather good bed bath. Now you really must stay for dinner."

"I'm afraid I can't at the moment. We must get to Paris."

"Paris? What fun. Do tell."

"Well this young chap, Clarence…" He grabbed the boys arm and pulled him forward. "… Is searching for his beloved."

"Really? I say, I do so enjoy a good love story."

"Yes," said Clarence, "She has been kidnapped and I believe her to be in Paris." Clarence could feel his voice changing as he spoke, almost straining to sound as posh as his hosts.

"Good lord. Then you really must get a move on."

"Shall I ready the train sir?" Said Pile in an almost exasperated tone as he seemed to magically appear from nowhere.

"Yes Pile. You must and make no bones about

it man."

"Very good sir."

Clarence looked back at Hogbert, "Train?"

"Yes. We have our own private locomotive, jolly swift she is too what." He pointed to the massive windows at the rear of the room as a steam train slowly moved into sight.

"Golly!" Said Clarence.

The steam train looked very much like the airship in that it was streamlined and had a very shiny black appearance with a fancy and very intricate pattern that covered the entire front half of the locomotive. As they walked towards the train Clarence noticed that there was an odd purple hue to the steam as it hissed from the sides of the engine and it felt strangely cold, like when he opened the fridges in the summer and would be engulfed in its 'dead mist' as he called it. But unlike the average steam train, there were odd pistons and bellows situated in various parts of the train's mechanism that pumped and breathed like tiny hearts and lungs, their purpose was unclear to Clarence as he examined the beast of a train but then he was never he'd been to sure on the anatomy of steam trains in the first place. Ace was already climbing all over the train as Harry stared whimsically at him, not sure of what to do with herself and her confused feelings that flapped about like confused butterflies in her tummy. Clarence wanted to feel that feeling, he wanted to look adoringly at somebody and for them to exchange the very same, unspoken but knowingly glance back, but that somebody was miles away and for now he would have to rely on the memory, and one particular memory struck out at him and sat in his head like a photograph.

As the train moved through the French countryside Clarence could still feel it, that embrace in his bedroom, she had told him to hold her tight and he had been so unsure and shy, but he bit his lip and felt angry for not showing that same warmth and tenderness.

"What's bothering ya Carlos?" Muttered the Clown from the other side of the carriage as he once again, completely forgot Clarences name.

"Oh nothing Clown, I'm just thinking about things being, well different," he sighed.

"Well you're not the only one kiddo. I have a lot of those thoughts…" And he pondered on those thoughts for a moment, "… I often think about the universe and its vastness and wonder if the gods are truly waiting in the sky for us at the end… And are they there to take our souls for an eternity in paradise or are we reborn to have another go at life?." He looked out of the window with a thoughtful frown and then looked back at Clarence and Harry. "And then I think. Who gives a bugger and I have another drink."

"Oh Clown you are a funny one."

He smiled his big, silly drunkards smile and stood up, "Right…I need to be sick. I told you travelling makes me all vomity."

As he staggered down the carriage, towards the toilets, Clarence watched with a smile. "You know, beneath that filthy drunk exterior there is a wonderful human being."

Harry leaned forward and placed a hand on the young mans knee, "We will find her you know Clarence."

"We will?" A deep pang of doubt bubbled away in Clarence's gut, troubling him deeply. "I just fear she has forgotten me."

"You are a very special person Clarence Bunn. She could not forget such a man and I am honoured to be making this journey with you."

"Really? You mean that?"

"Of course I do. If I hadn't have met you then I'd not have met Ace, and besides that, I'd never have made such wonderful new friends. You know, you have grown so much since I first met you. You have become brave and fearless and if I might say, your unshaven, rough and ready look really rather suits you." She winked and Clarence felt that familiar furnace feeling rise up from his neck.

"Golly," he fiddled with his fingers, "Can I ask you something Harry?"

"Of course you can Clarence."

"Well… it's like this." He felt his old stutter coming back like an unwelcome visitor, "I have a feeling in my gut whenever I think of Kelly and it makes me feel a little bit sick and… and I… I worry because I can't sleep or eat or even think straight for that matter."

Harry giggled, "That's love Clarence."

He felt the ball of relief unwind in his stomach and he sat back in his chair, "I didn't think it could happen so fast. We only had the weekend… and it wasn't even a whole weekend!"

"Clarence. I knew as soon as first saw Ace."

"So love at first sight does exist?"

Harry nodded, "I would've said no until the airport, but then it happened. Those eyes, that jaw, that accent… that body."

"Ok. Thank you Harry. That's quite enough of that," said Clarence uncomfortably, hurriedly trying to stop the conversation about Aces physique and avoiding anymore unnecessary blushing.

Harry laughed, "Oh you are silly. You shouldn't be embarrassed by it…" Harry frowned and leaned across, closer to Clarence, "Have you ever kissed a girl Clarence?"

"Well… I… Urm…" Here came that inevitable blush. He frantically tried to push it back down but to no avail and if anything, the attempt to reduce it only made it worse. He bumbled out some more words to make light of it all. "I was kissed once, but it was awful. She was like a plunger and I really didn't like it all."

Harry laughed and slapped Clarence on the knee, "Close your eyes Clarence."

"What?"

"You heard me. Shut them, relax and think of Kelly."

He obediently did as he was told. He sat back and shut his eyes. He could feel Harry moving forward, closer to his face and he gulped in fear that something horrid was going to happen, but then he felt it. Her soft lips touched his and a warm sensation flowed through his body like a rush of realisation. He opened his eyes slowly and saw Harry, inches away from his face, smiling softly. "Gosh!" But this time there was a different kind of breathlessness, "What was that?"

"That was a kiss Clarence."

"But why…"

Harry put a finger up to his mouth to silence him, "I want you to remember how soft that felt, and I want you to kiss Kelly like that when we find her ok?"

Clarence merely nodded with his mouth slightly open, "Uh huh."

"Now don't tell Ace about that or he will probably and quite literally kill you." She smiled as she turned and looked out of the window as if nothing had happened.

Suddenly Clown burst through the doors. "Are we there yet because we seem to be lacking toilet paper and I need a sh…"

"Its there," it's Clarence. And sure enough, over the horizon was the great city of Paris herself, "We're finally here," he whispered as his heart pumped excitedly, "I'm here Kelly."

Another night at the necromancers

The Parisian catacombs echoed with the chants as a small group uttered ancient words as they had done just days before beneath the city of Ashwood. The great mystic stood before his people with his arms raised, "And so brothers, we have come to this place. This place of death and magic and tonight we shall take the dead girl." Someone coughed, "Yes brother Hugo?"

"Well sir, it's like this. Where do we do the magic?"

"What?"

"Were do we do the magic? I thought the ancient scriptures' told of it happening in a far off land of dust?"

"Well… Yes but…" Stuttered the great mystic as he pondered the question, "The time is now brothers and the dead girl shall be with us within this night."

"But?" Said Hugo with his arm up.

"Brother Hugo! The Almighty One shall be here with the girl soon and then you can ask him your foolish questions yourself. In the mean time brothers, let us rejoice." Another hand came up from the back, "Yes brother?"

"It's sister actually. Sister Mavis."

"Yes sister Mavis?" He rolled his eyes

impatiently, "You have something to offer?"

"Well you keep on harping on about brother this and brother that but you never say sister…"

The great mystic rolled his eyes again, "Look, it's easier to say brothers than brothers and sisters ok?"

"Well I think it's sexist."

"Well you know what you can do then sister Mavis."

"I will then."

"Fine!"

"Fine!" She stood for a moment and then raised her hand, "Would you mind if I travelled back with you."

"Very well." Muttered the great mystic. "Does anyone else have any questions or quibbles or can I carry on?" He looked around the audience sternly, "Good! Now as you currently all seem to think this is a debate." He rolled his eyes as he spoke.

Another hand went up.

"Oh for goodness sake… Yes?" He snapped.

"So this is the necromancers right?"

"Yes?"

"Not the necrophilia group?"

"Absolutely not brother. Why that would be…"

The man began to back off into the darkness and the sound of his sandals echoed through the tunnels as he ran away.

 "Anybody else?" Called the great mystic to the now deathly silent and rather stunned room. "Good."

See you at the catacombs

Kelly had lost count of how many doctors and professors had examined her now, each one listening to her back and her chest in the vain attempt to find a heart beat. Torches shone in her eyes as tendon hammers bumped her knees and elbows. People had looked in her mouth and in her ears, some had even placed electrodes to her head, searching for some kind of impulse of life, but all the while, La Douche stood by her side like a protective fatherly figure. His right hand man Doctor Andrew stood close by too, his eyes flitting between a scrap of paper in his hands and then to the girl in wonder. She knew the blood results were back and she was almost definite that the paper in the Doctors possession held the numbers. Kelly feared they held her secret and worried about what could become of a girl with her past if it became common knowledge.

 "I think, gentlemen, that we shall call it a day now? Perhaps tomorrow we can discuss our findings and get the answers we seek eh?" La Douche eyed the others as some scribbled notes while others adjusted their glasses. "Mademoiselle Kelly is tiring." He placed a hand onto the girls shoulder and gave it a gentle squeeze.

Kelly looked up at him. He looked so grand and not half as frightening as he had on their first encounter. She felt safe with him and the Doctor and now something inside was aching to tell the secret, the deep dark enigma that hung in her like a frightful skeleton. Perhaps they would understand if she spoke out but the risk far outweighed the urge to tell and what if they were not to understand? Her secret would horrify them perhaps and then what? She thought again about the results, held by Doctor Andrew and she bit her lip and watched the room empty as La Douche shook hands with old friends. But after a brief discussion with Andrew he turned pale, something seemed wrong, his face looked pained as if he had heard a great sadness, and as he approached he crouched down onto one knee.

"My dearest Kelly. There is something you must know." He looked at the floor for a moment and placed his hand upon hers. "The blood results have told us a great dark piece of news. Doctor Andrew has told me that you appear to be dying?"

Kelly frowned and La Douche continued.

"Let me explain, it seems that your blood cells, although non functioning are, well, decaying. I believe that life itself is killing you."

Kelly stood and looked at Doctor Andrew, then around the empty room, "How? How long have I got?" It was all she could say and what did he mean? Would she just die, properly, like the other poor souls in this place?

Doctor Andrew grabbed her arm, "I couldn't say but the cells are decaying slower than normal. So perhaps we have time."

"Time for what Andrew?" Said La Douche.

The Doctor looked flustered and stuttered a little as he spoke, "Well I mean time to find a cure, or… or answers… or something?"

She could hear their voices now but in a muffled fuzz of noise. She rotated on the spot and could feel a strange haze coming over her like a black fog as the room began to close in on her. The feeling rushed up into her head and she felt a need within, unlike any other she had felt before, the need and sudden urge took hold of her and she ran, "I need some air," she called as she burst through the doors, down several flights of stairs and into the cold night. She ran and ran, not knowing where or why but she ran as fast as she could, pushing past couples and strangers alike, trying to escape the inevitable, frightening truth of her own new mortality. She stopped in a huge square with a fountain and looked up at the cherubs as they playfully spurted jets of water from their mouths. "Why?" She cried, "I just wanted to…" Her reflection in the water made her look distorted as the ripples moved the surface, creating a monster from the beautiful reflection. "…I just wanted to be among them father. That's all I wanted and now my death is dying." She feared this would happen but never actually believed it would, not really, not to her. If only she had listened to her father. He had warned her of it, he had told her she would never be able to live like one of them, not here beside them and never for this amount of time, but she was young and naïve to the reality of it all. She knew best, or so she had thought. Now it was too late and her father wouldn't be able to find her here in this foreign place. It would take something massive to find her and for the first time, in a long time, she just wanted her father.

Suddenly she noticed a small dog cocking it's leg against the wall of the fountain, it noticed her and appeared at her feet, wagging its stumpy, docked tail. She crouched down and stroked its head, "What's you name?"

 "Mr. Fluffles ma'am. And I…" The pause was genuine as the Clown tried to think of what to call himself. "Am Clown," slurred triumphantly, holding out a bottle wrapped in a brown paper bag, "Care for a little tipple miss?"

Kelly stood and looked at the funny dressed man as he staggered a little, "I don't, or rather can't drink but thank you Mr. Clown."

"Oh goodness no, thank you miss," he took a large glug from the bottle, "Means more for me," he hiccoughed.

Kelly giggled at the man, "You're English? What brings you to France? Are you in the circus?"

"Woo! Hold on little lady, that's too many questions in one go, Hic!" Clown pointed a finger at the girl and focused, "Yes I am English, well part welsh as it happens, but…Hic!… We don't talk about that," he winked, "And I don't work in the circus anymore, all dirty and corrupt and if I may say," He staggered, waving his finger about, "They were rather cruel to us different types."

"Oh you poor chap," said Kelly as she approached the Clown. "So the Circus left you here?"

The Clown hiccoughed, "No no, me and some chums came over on the train looking for someone."

Kelly felt a flutter in her stomach, "Who are you looking for?"

"Oh a girl I think… Yeshh, a girl."
Kellys eyes widened and she clasped her hands together, "Please Mr. Clown, who? Who are you with?"
The Clown puffed his cheeks out and blew out some alcohol, infused breath, "Clint!" He belched.
"Oh," she felt her non beating heart sink, "I just hoped it would be someone else."
Clown walked to her and placed his arm round her shoulder, "Tell you what kiddo. I know just how ya feel." He wiped his hand under his red nose, "I lost everyone close to me because I thought the circus was where I wanted to be. Had a gift ya see, used the cards to see the future, but the future I saw for me'self wasn't the future that happened. Bloody cards."
"That's very sad Mr. Clown, I mean, Clown."
"Yes it is. But sometimes a new future comes along and well, it's not as bad as the old future that you wanted in the past so you put the new future in the future the old future in the past… If that makes sense?" Even the Clown looked baffled by what he had just said and wondered what he was talking about.
Kelly looked at the floor, her future was still to be made, but it wasn't going to be the one she wished for either. She would have to accept her

fate now. "It's been jolly nice to meet you Mr. Clown but I really must be going."

"It has been nice to meet you too young lady."

"Oh please, it's Kelly."

The Clown froze, "I know that name." He thought as his drunken brain ticked like a bomb, with a thousand names rushing through it, names connecting to situations that in turn connected to… "You're the one we're looking for."

"What?"

"Yeah we came here to find the dead girl and her name is Kelly." Clown felt stunned that he had just remembered such details all at the same time, "Bloody hell," he said as he looked at the bottle to check what exactly he had been drinking.

"Are you here with Clarence"

"Yeah that's him… I think?."

Kelly ran at the Clown and flung her arms round him, lifting her feet of the ground with joy. "At last I can see him again. Please you must take me to him."

Clown put his thumb up, "You got it kiddo, let's skiddadle."

"Kelly? Step away from that filthy man at once," shouted Doctor Andrew as he appeared from the shadows, a revolver in his hand.

"Doctor Andrew? But he knows where Clarence is."

"Then, if he tells the truth, we will meet them in the morning in the catacombs."

The Clown frowned, "Okay doctor but no fancy business ok? Don't worry love, I'll bring him to ya."

The doctor leaned into Kelly slowly, "When I say run, we run ok?"

"But he knows Clarence."

"My dear girl, he is a Clown and Clowns come from the circus. Only Turnbuckle could be behind this."

Kelly realised that Doctor Andrew could be right. She wished it wasn't so but felt a little foolish for believing the Clown, "Ok," she whispered back.

But as they made their sudden run for it, a pair of dark shadows watched from the alleyways, moving together as one, watching the Clown, a glint of steel shone in the moon light and they both moved in towards the him.

The morning came and Kelly strolled between La Douche and Doctor Andrew. What if the Clown had been telling the truth? She would finally be meeting Clarence once again. But if it had been a lie then what? What would she do? Oh how she missed him so.

"My girl. You must be ready for disappointment," said La Douche as he pulled at her arm that was linked around his own, "Whatever happens, remember I will always be here for you."

Kelly placed her head against his arm and shut her eyes for a moment, hoping, praying to whichever god was listening, for a chance. And as they walked into the darkness of the catacombs, the girls eyes were drawn to the thousands of skulls that lined the walls. She felt a trickle like static electricity run up her spine and into her ears where it made a whispering sound, faint at first as voices slipped through the damp air.

"The place is up here," said the Doctor.

And there it was, the main hall of the catacombs. The place was magnificent and Kelly could feel the death around her like being surrounded by old friends and family.

"Well? Where is this Clown fellow eh?" Said the Frenchman.

Andrew turned and pointed a finger beyond La Douche, "My gods. Look out."

But it was too late as a blade poked through La Douches shoulder. He turned and drew the sword from his cane, "Run Kelly, run."

Kelly did as she was told and barged passed

Doctor Andrew, knocking him to the ground.

La Douche swished the sword through the air, "Show yourself coward." The wound had merely pierced the flesh but it still hurt like the devil and this angered La Douche to the core. He hated cowards at the best of times but being attacked from behind was below cowardice, "Well. Step from the darkness and fight me like a man."

A figure moved forward and it startled the Frenchman. A man pranced forward, his face, white with paint and three black tear drops upon his cheek. He danced and twiddled his skinny legs in their tight black leggings, "Shhh," said the mime, placing his finger to his lips.

"A mime? Is this some kind of joke?" He turned slightly to Doctor Andrew, "Go with Kelly. Make sure she is safe." Andrew did as he was told and ran to the opposite side of the domed room, but then he stopped and turned. He watched for a while from the shadows, where no one else could see him. A malign smile crept over his face and his eyes narrowed as he saw the mime move around the room, acting out a performance as if he were behind glass and slowly he slid back into the gloom, in pursuit of the dead girl.

La Douche swiped his sword at the mime,

cutting a thin strip into his black and white striped top, "Get back or the next one will be fatal!"

The mime merely looked startled and placed a hand over it while pretending to fall backwards as if dying. Suddenly he thrust a hand forward, throwing a thin stiletto knife at La Douche. It sunk into the mans abdomen and he stumbled back, "You will never get her Turnbuckle."

A slow round of applause echoed from behind the mime and the ring master revealed himself. "Well done Frenchy. You have foiled me again, but alas, now you will die. And how ironic that it should be in a tomb."

"What is this? You have sent this… this thing, to kill us?"

"Oh no La Douche. This is just for you. The Doctor is nothing to me so if he dies, well, so be it. But the girl?" He stroked his moustache, "Hmm, she is another story all together."

The mime spun a knife on his finger as he watched La Douche bleed.

"My mime wants to kill you La Douche and I want you dead. So what do you suggest?"

La Douche stood proudly and puffed out his chest, "By now Kelly is far away and the Doctor is with her. He has a gun you know."

Turnbuckle raised his fingers patronisingly to

his mouth, "Ooh a gun? Scary," he laughed once and suddenly his faced turned to that of pure hatred, "You almost ruined me La Douche and now it's your time to be ruined."

"Come and get me," said the Frenchman and he charged, sword readied at the pair.

The dark tunnels of the Parisian catacombs spread out like veins beneath the city. A million skeletons filled the vast expanse due to the overcrowded grave yards up above and every skull seemed to call out at Kelly as she ran past them. The ground beneath her feet was hard and cold but every now and then she would splash through a puddle that soaked into her shoes and dress. She stopped in a small opening and stood, awestruck. The entire place was covered in human bones, even the domed ceiling was adorned with the dead. She rotated on the spot as the silent screams of a million souls called out at her. She could hear every one of them, loud and clear in her mind and in her ears. "What do you want from me?" She called, "I'm not him…" But the voices never answered her, they just pulled at her soul with invisible hands. They knew who she was and where she had come from and they wanted something that she couldn't give them. The dome began to move around her as the spirits themselves started to flow from their skeletons in a spiral of phantoms. Kelly crouched down with her hands over her head, "Please stop. I don't know how to help you." She felt them brushing past her hair with their ghostly finger tips and whispering to her. She couldn't make out what they were saying, but their voices were desperate, for what, she wasn't sure but they needed her to do something for them. Slowly Kelly held out her arms and she felt the spirits seeping through her fingers like cold, black sand, some even tugged at her sleeves but she stood firm. A dark mass of phantoms swirled before her, creating what appeared to be a portal of dark light, Kelly looked into it and through the haze of black she saw a figure, it beckoned at her with a bony finger. "Mortis." It's voice was that of a thousand voices, some whispered while others screamed but all spoke in one voice to the girl. It beckoned again as it repeated itself, "Mortis."

 Kelly walked to the portal and tilted her head, listening to the voices and watching the spiralling darkness, but then thoughts of Clarence came to her and now she backed away from the figure. The voice spoke louder now, almost demanding the girl to enter the swirling black vortex, but how could she go?

Leaving her Clarence without an explanation or even a goodbye would surly break his heart she thought, "Not now," she called, pausing for a second, and then whispering, "Not now."
"Kelly. Thank goodness I've found you. I was terrified you had been lost in this godforsaken place," gasped Doctor Andrew as he stumbled breathlessly into the room.

"Oh I don't know. It's not so bad here," she said as her eyes darted round at the now silent skeletons.

"Who were you talking to just now?"

"Oh… I was just thinking aloud is all."

"Come now, we must get out of here before they catch up with us." He grabbed her arm but Kelly resisted. "Come on girl, we have no time to waste," his voice now agitated and uncharacteristically aggressive.

"Where is François?"

Andrew lowered his head, "I'm afraid he gave his life for us… For you."

Kelly had that feeling in her gut as she looked down the dark tunnel from where she had come from. He had been like a father figure to her and now he was gone from her life like all the other things she had loved. Taken from her so cruelty. "Maybe I can help him, bring him back..." She whispered.

Suddenly footsteps could be heard running from the darkness before them and Kelly backed away, behind the Doctor, "Is it the murderer?"

Doctor Andrew smirked, "No…" He grabbed the girls arm and pulled her forward as a group of robe wearing men rushed into sight, "…They are my friends, the Necromancers."

In for the long haul

Clown lay on the Hotel room sofa with his feet up and Harry at his head holding a cold flannel on the egg sized lump that could be seen clearly beneath his grease painted face. "You were very lucky they only did this to you Clown. It could have been a great deal worse," said the Highway woman.

"Well they took me by surprise this time, but if I'd have known they were there I'd have…" Clown winced as a fresh cold flannel was placed onto his head. "…They were lucky I wasn't ready for um though, I'll tell ya that for nothing." He made a pained expression and took full advantage of further mollycoddling from Harry.

Clarence stood in the bathroom, straightening his tie again and called out to his friend, "So you're sure it was Kelly then?"

"Yep. Was defiantly her kiddo," said Clown. Clarence untied his tie and restarted again and now even his butterflies had butterflies of excitement as he thought of seeing Kelly again, "Are you sure?"

Clown laughed but winced as he grabbed his ribs, "I best stay here. Bleedin' painful bruises you know."

"You will be ok here on your own won't you?"

Said Harry as she stood up, away from the injured funny man.

Clown held a bottle of French brandy tight to his chest, "We should be ok I think."

Clarence walked out into the lounge and straightened his tie one last time, "How do I look?"

Harry nodded her approval and Ace put a thumb in the air, "She's gonna love it buster."

"Clown?" Said Clarence, "Have you ever been to Transylvania?"

"Nope. Why do ask Clive?"

"Oh you just mentioned it a few times when you got back before, after your fight with those ruffians."

"Yeah, ain't that where those monsters come from?" Said Ace as he looked down the barrel of a freshly polished revolver.

Clown remained on the sofa, thinking hard, "I have been around but never there. Must've been another one of me visions," he said, in a most matter of fact manner.

Clarence crouched down, "Visions?"

"Yeah I get um from time to time. Don't know what I'm saying but usually means something." Again speaking as if there was nothing abnormal about what he was saying.

Clarence stood and looked around at his

friends. A very uneasy feeling swamped his gut as he thought about what the Clown had said, "We must leave." He grabbed his coat from the back of the chair, "Now."

 The catacombs were silent and dark as the Clarence, Harry and Ace made their way through the walkways. "Kelly!" Called Clarence, "Are you here?" Something caught his eye through the gloom and he rushed forward in hope of it being her, "Kelly?" He called again. But as he neared the figure he could see it was La Douche. "Where is she you scoundrel?"
 "Monsieur Bunn. I am so sorry," he staggered into the young mans arms and the pair fell to their knees.
 "Mr La Douche. What ever happened?"
 "It was a set up. Turnbuckle and his hideous mime and now I fear that not all is as it seemed."
 "But what of Kelly? Is she ok?" Clarence grabbed him by the collar of his coat.
 "I believe she is safe but know this…" He coughed and a trickle of blood ran from his mouth, "… In the end I realised that she is just like you and I but also unlike any other." He smiled at Clarence and gripped his hand, "I am sorry Clarence. If I had not taken her, then

none of this would ever have happened." He coughed again and clutched his abdomen.

"Monsieur La Douche. Please. Where are they now? Where are they going?"

"We were supposed to stay here in Paris for further tests, to save her."

"What? To save her? From what?" Clarence felt his heart pounding in his chest as if it were trying to escape.

"Oh dear Clarence, she is dying. I am truly sorry."

"But she can't die. She is already dead."

"There is a man in Romania. We were going to see him next… he is an expert in this sort of phenomena apparently. He has an artefact."

"Romania? But that's where… La Douche?"

But the Frenchman had gone. His life had slipped away from his body like a pick-pocketed purse, silent and with no one noticing until it was too late.

Clarence began to cry, uncontrollably although he gritted his teeth to evade the tears, they just couldn't be stopped from running down his cheeks.

"What the heck was he talking about buddy?" Said Ace as he crouched down with a hand on the lads shoulder.

Clarence turned and looked at his friend, "I'm

sorry. I never told you. Kelly is dead."

Ace scratched his head, "What?"

Harry merely frowned as the lad stood, "Clarence you need to explain to Ace," she demanded.

"It was one night in the mortuary. She was there and dead and then… and then she wasn't but they came and took her. And now she is here but isn't and La Douche is dead and I've lost her again." He began to weep uncontrollably again and Harry ran to him, throwing her arms round him.

Ace still looked confused but said nothing. He wasn't the type of guy who got mixed up in emotional situations so he stood back, keeping his distance until everyone had stopped crying. He thought for a moment and nodded once to himself, "We'll find her bud, you can count on it. No matter what it takes, I'm with ya'all the way." He nodded again to himself, knowing that he had said the right thing in a difficult situation. Not bad he thought to himself.

"But Romania?" Said Clarence in a torrent of tears and snot, "It's a scary place, I've heard it's filled with monsters and the like."

"Well maybe that's a kinda good thing being that she's dead an all," bumbled Ace in a most non helpful way.

Harry glared at him in the manner that any man would recognise as 'that look' and he realised then that perhaps the silent option would be the favoured method from now on, well until the dust had settled at least.

Clarence sniffed and snivelled and looked up through a haze of tears, "She was here and we missed her. We must go to Romania." He looked at Ace, "You said no matter what. Did you mean it?"

Ace saluted at his friend. He may not have been the most emotionally charged or switched on of men but he knew one thing and that was the importance of friendship. "You bet ya life on it Clarence."

Dance macabre

La Douches airship rose high into the air and Kelly watched the city of Paris disappear into a toy town land below her. She wished she could cry for La Douche and for Clarence, but her tears remained dry. That empty promise of seeing him again had been the final straw and now her heart sunk like a rock in the sea, but something appeared strange about the Clown that night, he hadn't seemed wicked or malicious, and when she had hugged him she could feel his heart pounding in his chest. Kelly heard the sound of running outside the door but ignored the words and the shouting, things were getting a bit too strange now and someone was lying to her and all fingers were now pointing at Doctor Andrew.

The lights of the city became grey, moon lit countryside as they made their way east towards the border, and Kelly could make out the shape of a steam train below, puffing its way in the same direction as the airship. Its carriages lighting the ground around it as it roared through the fields like a massive black snake. A silhouette could be seen in one of the windows, standing lonesome with one hand pressed against the glass, something seemed so sad about the figure that Kelly couldn't keep from staring as it became distant and then vanished into a tunnel.

Clarence stood in the train carriage with a hand against the window, still staring at the part of the sky where the airship had been minutes before they had entered the tunnel. Something had been odd about it, perhaps it had been the silhouette in the window way above that had gripped him, and now he wondered who it had been and if they had seen him. Perhaps they felt the same pain as he did right now and shared the same feeling of utter hopelessness. His palm slowly became a fist and he slammed it against the window and turned to Harry, "Teach me to shoot."

The highway woman looked out from under her hat, blinking out of her sleep and looking a little cross about it, "Eh?" She snarled.

Clarence never normally spoke in such a tone and now a surprised young Mr. Bunn immediately corrected himself, "I mean… Sorry to wake you but please, could you teach me to shoot?"

Harry stretched and sat upright, "Clarence, why on earth would you want to learn to shoot?"

"Because I'm going to kill whoever has Kelly."

She removed her hat and placed it on her lap,

"You know it's not always violence that gives you revenge. I should know."

"But look at the pain they've caused. Surely that counts for something?" He scratched his head, "And I feel so… so cross."

"Oh my dear Clarence, I once lost someone very close to me and thought that killing her murderer was the only way forward…" She looked down and fiddled with her hat, "But his death at my hand never brought my sister back and I still feel the same pain as I did then. Please think carefully Clarence."

He sat swiftly in front of Harry and took her hand, "I'm sorry, I didn't know."

"How were you too know?... Clarence, since we first met I have come to realise what a wonderful, kind friend I have found in you and this is why I can't let you ruin everything by killing whoever it is."

"Guys!" Called Ace as he stomped down the carriage, breaking the moment like a plane crash, "We're almost there."

Clarence looked up at his friend and smiled but something seemed odd, something he couldn't quite put his finger on, and then it hit him like a brick of revelation concealed in a Billy club of frightful total realisation. He stood sharply, and for a moment with his mouth wide open he stared at the American. "Who's driving the train?"

The great Effing house mansion was lit up like a fairytale castle and as the train hissed to a halt, Clarence jumped down and walked to the engine. "Yee gads!" He gasped, "Clown?"
 The sight was almost frightful if it had not been so ridiculous. There in the cab of the train was the Clown with a drivers hat pulled snugly over his curly red wig. Beside him sat the terrier Mr. Fluffles, also sporting a drivers cap, albeit a smaller version. He pulled on the chain that sounded the trains whistle and called, "Whoop whoop," as he beamed with delight while his dog yapped with joy.
 "I wouldn't have believed it if I hadn't seen it with my own eyes," said Clarence as he assisted the funny man from the train.
 "It's a childhood dream of mine you know. I've always wanted to drive a train." His eyes were filling up with tears as he spoke.
 There was a strong smell of whiskey on the mans breath and Clarence considered how legal it was to drive a train with a head full of alcohol, let alone how safe it was. But, drunk or not, he had done a grand job of driving the train and Clarence could not help but admire his

friends new found talent.

 Hogbert rushed out to greet his friends, swiftly followed by the man servant Pile who held a tray of drinks precariously atop of his raised arm. "So? Did you find the girl?" Chirped the millionaire.

 Clarence shook his head solemnly, "She was there… but we lost her again."

 "Oh that's jolly bad luck old boy." He patted the lad on the shoulder in an attempt to sooth the situation but nothing was about to help how Clarence felt. "Come in, you really must rest."

 Inside and the mansion was a state of busyness, with maids and footmen decorating the walls with fancy bows and garlands. "It's all for the masked ball this evening, do say you'll come."

 "I think I'll stay in my room thank you all the same," murmured Clarence as he slopped off ahead with Pile. He looked to his side as three men entered from the servants quarters, they appeared to be musicians judging by the instrument cases they carried, but Clarence was more interested in their faces. He knew he had seen the three of them somewhere before. "Who are those gentleman Pile?"

 The butler looked down his nose at the men, "Oh they are just the entertainment sir. Danse

Macabre quartet I believe they call themselves."

"Dance of the dead?" Whispered Clarence.

"Yes I believe so, much like the classical piece sir."

"Should there not be a forth if it's a quartet?" Clarence whispered to himself as he watched Pile walk ahead and up the white, marble staircase as he began to hum the tune Danse Macabre.

"That poor boy. Is there nothing can be done for him?" Said Harry

Clown bumbled forward between her and Ace with a glass of Champaign in each hand, "Tell ya what he needs…" He slurped on the first glass and slurred. "…A good drink, a good shleeps." The second glass disappeared in one gulp. "…and then a right good fu..."

"That's quite enough of that thank you Mr. Clown," interrupted Harry.

The couple of hours sleep seemed to help and now young Clarence walked through the corridors admiring the many paintings that lined the walls, in fact there were so many portraits that they could be mistaken for an odd but rather colourful looking wall paper with their frames giving the walls a somewhat three dimensional appearance. He could hear the three man Quartet downstairs as their music whispered throughout the building and he felt himself humming to it's mysterious and haunting tune as if it's chords and melodies were somehow hypnotising him into humming along to a tune he had never heard. A woman suddenly giggled and ran past him, closely followed by a young gentleman into one of the rooms. So many rooms thought Clarence walking past the door as it slammed shut. He wondered why one would need so many rooms, he lived out of just one room and that was plenty for him, but then this house held so many grand parties with many guests of the highest class. He wondered what it must be like to live in such a grand mansion with a rich upbringing and the freedom to come and go as you pleased. Clarence stopped at the library, it was huge and he was sure he had never seen so many books in his entire life. Books, rows upon rows of books, all of various sizes and colours, from floor to ceiling and spreading out into the darkest corners of the room, books. Their papery bodies muffled the sounds from elsewhere and the lad felt suddenly safe within the library's dense forest of knowledge. He ran a hand across the spines as he walked down an isle and felt their different textures, every one of them so individual and some so rare and expensive that even just one of them could buy him his own house in the upper streets of Ashwood. He imagined himself and Kelly together in a town house, looking out over the city with its chimneys and its barrow boys shouting in the markets square. He saw a door opening and Harry and Ace visiting them with a baby or two and there was Clown with Mr. Fluffles and he was sober and how they all laughed at their adventures. But then he realised that his dream was far from the reality, and in fact, he wondered if he would ever see Kelly again. His fingers suddenly brushed past a book and the spine caught his finger, slicing the skin a little. He placed the wounded digit in his mouth and sucked the blood from its tip. "Bugger," He said as he looked at the offending book. Its title caught his eye, "The occult and macabre art of Necromancy?" He slid the book from the shelf and blew several years worth of dust from it, wondering when it had last been taken from it's home on that shelf. On closer inspection it seemed to be older than the others and it's cover felt almost leathery and if he didn't know better he would have imagined it to be made from human skin. He shuddered and opened the book to the front page of contents.

He read down the sections and came to a paragraph that read, 'The spell of ever life, by prior Philipe De Caske' He shuddered again with a chill that seemed to stay up his spine for a little longer than welcomed as he thumbed through the pages. Each word had been hand written in the most beautiful calligraphy and he imagined an old monk sitting by candle light as he began to read the first lines…
January 3rd
 "For at the first day I had taken my black robe and felt it's majic. It's ancient origins I could not begin to imagine but know this, it has such mystic powers that it could only be sent from the gods themselves…or from the ones of the underworlds."
February 19th
 "And so I took the great staff of Mahooganooba and stood in the red hue of the blood moon with the dead girl. She did not know what was her intended fate but she was ready to exchange her living and eternal death for my mortality. Her love guided her if nothing more."
February 20th
 "Alas the spell did not work and I fear that now the time has passed by. Perhaps there was something else needed, but yet as I write I

cannot help but feel a betrayal in our tight community."

February 24th

 "My suspicions were correct and I have had word that brother Lupine had stolen a third Artefact and taken it to a remote place in Romania. At least we, the Brothers of the seventh moon, have the robe and the staff."

March 1st

 "My final entry. The time has passed and so, I am saddened to say, has the dead girl. Her soul is now rested and we must wait for the next revolution of the prophecy.

…Clarence sat on the floor with his mouth wide open, words could not begin to explain his emotions as he stared at the page. The rest of the book was filled with scrawling and pictures of rituals, but no more did it mention the dead girl. Was it her? What was Kelly and had it been her all those years before? He shivered again and shut the book hard as a million and one thoughts whizzed around his mind making him feel giddy with it. It seemed that the crazy old witch in the woods of Cobblers Knob was right about the Necromancers. They must be the ones after Kelly, but who where they he thought. La Douche was dead and to be fair to the old man, and to his own admission, was just a scientist. Then there was that hideous ringmaster, Maurice Turnbuckle. He was after Kelly but again, his only motive had been the money. Clarence scratched his head, perhaps the Necromancers were a hidden society who were working under cover of darkness, or maybe they were not even involved and the witch had just happened to have read the same book as he had just read… he thought for a moment about how ridiculous that thought had been and stood up with the book under his arm. "Party time," he said to himself as he left the library.

From the top of the staircase Clarence could see the whole room and he watched for a moment. He eyed the three man quartet with suspicion and they seemed to notice him too as they played on to the packed ballroom, with its masked gentlemen and elegant ladies, dancing and twirling like graceful sprites. In the corner he could see Ace and Harry almost wrapped around each other and there was the Clown with a group of very posh looking ladies, laughing and clapping at the dancing Mr. Fluffles. He rubbed his unshaved chin and adjusted his bowtie as he walked down the stairs into the flurry of bodies and seemed to move majestically with them to make his way to the other side of the room to where Lord Flemington-Ward stood.

"Mr Bunn. How absolutely wizard that you could make it. I've just been talking with my guests Lord and Lady Bottomly about you old chap."

Clarence nodded at the couple and held out the book, "I found this in the library. I wondered if you could explain it to me."

Hogbert placed his monocle over his right eye and examined the book, "Well I say. Haven't seen this old thing in a while." He looked about the room for a moment and then pointed to a small gentleman, "My old chum Earl Pratt." He leaned into the lads ear and whispered, "The Earl is a devil with all that occult malarkey you know. Used to practice a bit myself what." He waved at the man, "Ooh," he called, "Old bean. This is my jolly good friend Clarence. Found this book in the library. What's it all about?"

Clarence watched the posh folk for a moment and wondered why they had to talk in short shape sentences. The Earl fingered through the book and puffed on a very elegant looking cheroot. "I say. This is an original Necromancers diary."

Clarence pushed a few pages away and revealed the part he had been so shocked by.

"This bit. I read it and wondered if it was going to happen again." The words rushed from his lips as he tried desperately to sound calm, but the boys heart raced in its need to know the truth, a truth that was so close but so far out of reach.

"Well I do believe it might just happen again if I'm honest. However…"

But the lad interrupted, "Sorry but what about the dead girl it mentions there? The dead girl, there." His finger pointing to the words 'dead girl' on the page.

"Hmm. I recall a few passages I read a while back about an apparent rising of the dead. Something that happened about that time as I remember. Was rumour of it happening again by all accounts."

"Who is she?"

"Well I'm not too sure old boy. Some say she was conjured up by Necromancers where as others believe she is the incarnation."

"Incarnation? Of what?" Clarence couldn't hold the desperation from his voice any longer.

The Earl laughed and patted Clarence on the shoulder. "Death of course. The old Grim Reaper what."

Clarence stood silent as the Earl and lord Flemington-Ward continued to laugh and go about their own conversation. The world about him felt as if it was closing in as masked faces looked and laughed with pointing fingers and cake in their mouths. He spotted the table with a roasted pigs head on it and the apple within its mouth and a feeling of nausea gripped his stomach. Someone passed him a glass of wine and he drank it in one but the feeling didn't go away and so he grabbed another from a tray and another from the hand of a footman as the world began to spin around him like a carousel. He pushed through the hordes of party goers, trying to escape the madness as it washed over him like a wave. The music, the laughter, the noise, it was all too much and his mind throbbed with the very idea that his Kelly was some how a living, but dead, incarnation of the Grim Reaper. He ran to a set of doors and through a corridor that led to more doors and corridors, but the music still followed him, grabbing at him and whistling its high pitched violins into his ears. But now the music turned to noise, making him feel sick with its screams and squeals and he could see the pigs head in his mind and the apple and the blood. He reached a final door and as it burst open a wall of ice cold fresh air hit him and he fell to his knees. His fingers pressed against the snow and he vomited.

"Ah there's a good lad. Bring it up kiddo," said a very familiar voice of the Clown who was just zipping up his trousers and puffing on a very large cigar.

"I'm so confused Clown," said Clarence just before he vomited again.

"Well," began Clown as he pulled another cigar from his pocket and passed it to Clarence. "Its something that happens to every boy at a certain age. Girls or boys? You can't decide but if you want to chat about… Urm… Things, then."

He snatched the cigar from his friend and looked at it, "No Clown. It's about Kelly."

"Oh! Thank gods," he wiped his brow, "But yes, of course. She is a pretty one Christopher."

"Who are the Necromancers Clown?" He plonked himself back into the snow, "I mean I know what they do but who are they? I need to find them because I think they have Kelly."

Clown riffled in his coat and pulled out a deck of cards, "Say no more kiddo. Lets ask the cards." He shuffled them and then dropped them across the ground. "No! Leave them, it's fate what did that." And he picked them back up, noticing the top card. "See the bloody death card again…" Suddenly he phased out, but this time his eyes turned white.

"Clown? Clown? Are you alright?"

"Yeeees. The girl… She is taken by… by…"

"By who darn it?" Said Clarence sounding a little American.

"A trusted professional…?"

Clarence scratched his head, "Well the only doctor I know is… Oh my gosh."

Clown phased back in and staggered a little, "What did I say?"

"Is it Doctor Andrew? Is it him?"

"Is who, who?" Slurred Clown as he wobbled on his feet a little.

"Never mind Clown."

"Sorry Clifford."

"It's ok." But it wasn't ok and Clarence began to put his puzzle together, but unfortunately the pieces didn't match up and however hard he tried, there was no way they would connect in his mind. If it was the doctor then why was he never seen and why was he so nice. And besides, he could've taken Kelly long before, on transit to the Mortuary even. If it had been Turnbuckle then fair enough, or even Penny Dreadful but the Doctor? The whole of his adventure whizzed round and round in his head but nothing made any sense and then there was Hogbert and the Earl. What if it was one of them? What if it was all some kind of plan, controlled by some mysterious higher power.

"Can I try something with you?" Announced Clown suddenly.

"What?"

"Close your eyes and relax Cecil."

Clarence thought about this for a moment, the last time he had been asked to close his eyes and relax he had been kissed and a little part of him worried if the clown had the same intentions. But he did as he was told and closed his eyes.

"You are getting shleepy," slurred Clown.

Slowly Clarence felt himself drift off into a strange waking sleep. He was perfectly aware of his surroundings and the Clown before him but he felt as if he was dreaming. He could see through a haze in the distance, a figure walking towards him. It was La Douche. "You're dead he whispered."

"Oui. I am dead, but my soul travels through the mists of time and space, life and death."

"But what is it you want La Douche?"

"I av, how you say, information on these Necromancers."

"You do?" Clarence suddenly felt himself lift up, out of his own body like a ghost and glide through the air, through the oblivious Clown and towards the spiritual Frenchman. A glance back saw his body sitting in a trance-like state in the snow, eyes wide and white, almost dead-like. "Then please help me." The words hissed from his spiritual lips like a dream, with no audible sound but the thought and feeling was there.

"My murderer was not the mime or even the ring master but my friend. I trusted him and he stabbed me in the back… quite literally."

"So it is Doctor Andrew? He's a Necromancer."

"No Monsieur Bunn, he is THE Necromancer and now he seeks the final piece for the ritual."

"What ritual? What are they planning to do? I'm confused."

"They will go to a place. A place to the east of here in Romania and they will collect the final fragment… Then the ritual will take place where the after life is celebrated."

"What is this place you speak of?" Shouted Clarence silently.

But his words went nowhere and fell on the ears of no one as slowly La Douche vanished into nothingness and Clarence felt himself floating back into himself and becoming conscious once more. "What happened Clown?"

"I dunno. You tell me kiddo."

"I saw La Douche and he warned me about Doctor Andrew."

"Ah death…!" Clown waved a knowing finger in the air, "…And Necromancers. I bloody knew it."

"So the final piece of the puzzle is in Romania then?"

"Is that what the ol' Frenchy said?"

"Yes. He said something about a final fragment. I think he means that we need to get it before they do."

"Then I guess that's where we need to go next then Clinton."

"Clown?" He licked his lips and could taste something odd, "You didn't kiss me did you?"

Roaming in Romania

Romania, with its rolling hills and beautiful countryside were much to the surprise of Kelly as the airship landed. She had half expected to see darkness and creepy forests, not the picturesque view that met her as she disembarked. "It's beautiful." She said as she breathed in the fresh air. She closed her eyes and for a moment she was in another place, somewhere that wasn't with strangers but somewhere with the one she loved. She envisaged herself running through the fields and rolling down the hills, laughing, just as she had imagined this life to be in the first place. But it had all been a very romantic idea and nothing like she had wished. No fun and frolics, no sunshine and singing. Why had she believed this to be so? Why had she believed this world of the living to be such a fun and exciting place? But it was all too late for her now, she was stuck in a cold, dark world with people who wanted to harm her.

Doctor Andrew stepped out beside the girl, knocking her from her day dream and produced a map from his coat. He examined it for a moment, then pointing towards a dip between two hills he said, "We need to go there. That's where the artefact is and then we can save you." He looked at the girl and tried his best to appear as sincere, but she could see through it. It had been the very same look she had seen in the eyes of Turnbuckle. Those lying, selfish eyes that hid nothing but greed and dishonesty.

A large group of men had also disembarked from the airship with boxes and bags, ready for what looked to be a long journey. A few of them had rifles over their shoulders and Kelly began to wonder what exactly this trip was going to entail.

The ground was hard and frozen but the sun felt warm on the back of the girls neck as they walked towards the woods. Kelly felt anxious as they neared the trees, something didn't feel right at all and she knew they were about to make a grave mistake by entering the forest. "We mustn't go in there," she said, stopping at the edge of the tree line.

Doctor Andrew grabbed her wrist, "Don't be foolish girl. There is nothing more in these woods but trees and squirrels for goodness sake."

"There is a lot more in there than you can imagine, I can feel it," snarled the girl with a fearless glint in her eye, "It doesn't want us in there. It's evil."

He pulled on her wrist, "I don't care what you say, we need to go through here so shut up and be a good girl will you?"

The deeper into the forest they trekked, the heavier the shrubs and plants got. The trees and their branches seemed to leer at the group as they wandered through the tiny tracks and dense thicket and a large man walked ahead, cutting the way clear with a machete. "See. Nothing but bloody trees," said the doctor as he yanked on Kelly's arm.

But the sound of howling broke the silence and tranquillity of the wood, the birds above stopped singing and the group stopped instantly in their tracks. "What the bloody hell was that?" Called a man as he pulled his rifle up against his chest. "Was it a wolf?"

"Wolves as well as squirrels? Sounded more like a monster to me," hissed the girl with a venomous look in her eyes, "I told you."

The doctor laughed and gestured about him, "These men have guns. Monsters have claws and Wolves have paws." But no sooner had the words left his lips than one of his group disappeared into the undergrowth with a muffled scream. A gun shot echoed through the forest as another man vanished without a trace.

"Stay calm gentlemen and keep your eyes peeled." The man directly in front of the doctor suddenly lost his footing and vanished too. The doctor pulled a hand gun from his coat and fired three shots into the area where his comrade had gone but still the ground moved. "Change of plan gentlemen… RUN!" And with that, the forest seemed to move, not from Andrews men though, but from something a lot more sinister and a great deal bigger than the men who were now running for their lives. Another man shouted as his partner was dragged into the dark woodland. He pulled on his friends hands as the blood curdling screams filled the air but his strength couldn't match up to the unseen thing. "It's the plants… Oh by the gods… They're alive!" He shouted, but his words where wasted as at that very same moment two roots burst from the ground and took him by the throat, pulling him away from his comrade and to his unknown fate. Doctor Andrew and Kelly didn't look back as they ran and several others followed, but the screams of many more of the group filled the dense woods and echoed like a haunting reminder of their deaths.

 "I told you," said a now smug Kelly as they reached a road at the other side of the forest, "I said we shouldn't go through there."

 Andrew struck the girl across the cheek with the back of his hand, "Don't you think I know that now? Do you think I enjoyed seeing my friends die back there?" His words were now sincere and his voice shaky as he wiped some saliva from his bottom lip.

Kelly rubbed her face and a slight feeling of pain crept through to the surface, but she scowled at the man and although he was saddened by his loss, Kelly could still only see the brute that was now Doctor Andrew. A couple more men emerged from the trees but the party was now less than half its original size and those who had made it through were either injured or stunned and pale from fear of what they had just encountered.

 A man stumbled from the bushes, his body and limbs were covered with wounds where the plants and roots had lashed at him like whips. He fell to his knees, his voice raspy and dry from all the screaming. "Sir. They're all dead, all of them…" And then his soul seemed to just vanish from him as his lifeless body flopped to the ground.

 "What does he mean, all of them?" Whispered Kelly.

 Doctor Andrew walked among the now

depleted group, shaking his head. "He meant La Douches team. None of them have survived." He pulled the map from his coat and ran his finger across the parched, yellow paper. "Just through this track and we shall be there." His voice so matter of fact now as if nothing had happened. A large flying bug landed on his arm and he watched with curiosity as it too inspected his skin curiously. "La Douche would have loved it here. All these funny little animals and plants." He slowly picked the bug from his arm and watched as its legs wiggled in an attempt to escape the man's fingers. "But he isn't… He's dead." And with those words, his fingers tensed and the insect popped, dribbling it's yellow internal juices down the Doctors wrist. He smiled at Kelly as he wiped his hand across the front of his waistcoat, "Just like you."

__Lucky we had a Clown__

The Slipstream zoomed through the sky leaving a purple vapour trail behind it like the tail of a comet. It's occupants remained silent this time, no one spoke, they all stared ahead or out of the window at the landscape beneath them as it flashed past like an oil painting, blurred green and grey across its canvas. Clarence looked at his friends. How his life had changed from the days growing up at Wilkomsirs family morticians. He could almost recall as far back as his father, but only a faint and distant memory dwelt in his mind. He remembered a large man in dark ragged clothing and a bowler hat sitting in a bare room at a table, a bottle in his hand and drops of whisky running down his stubbly chin as he shouted at the frightened boy. That had been his father as he could remember, the smell of booze and cigarettes. The violence and the noise that filled his head with a pain like no other, the emotional pain of hopelessness that no child should ever have to feel. He thought hard and could only just find the first day with Angus Wilkomsir in his mind. The cakes and the family and the stares, the sad, pitying stares. A policeman had been there too, shaking his head and pointing at the small boy. Then the days of a growing Clarence caught up with him and he remembered running through the streets with other boys chasing, mocking him for being the boy who was lost in a bet. They would never hit him but in a way, Clarence almost wished the attacks had been physical. At least then the pain would have been on the outside, with disappearing bruises instead of the mental scars that would constantly burn his confidence away. The flash backs of being curled up in corner with shouts and laughter directed at him angered him, why could he never stand up for himself like everyone else? But then his teenage years had been just as abusive with Mr Wilkomsir treating him like a slave in that place. It wasn't the Scotsman's fault though, it was his upbringing too, but it didn't help the lad and by then he had already given up on trying to better himself. His life answering to Mr Wilkomsir and being the boy that helps out. Clarence had, on more than one occasion, contemplated ending his life, but he couldn't even do that, so his life went on, unchanging… That was until he had met Kelly. She had been like a silvery ray of light into his dreary world. Waking his inner self and making him realise that there was more to life, there really was something called happiness and it really could exist for him. And now, there in that cabin, he was surrounded by new friends, true friends who where willing to go this far for him, risking it all in the name of friendship. He had never felt such feelings in all of his life before, this feeling of acceptance and it had all been down to Kelly, because if not for her then Clarence would still be at the Morticians. A smile appeared on his face, the type of smile that was sent from the subconscious and almost impossible to hide.

"Hazah!" Called Hogbert as the airship banked and slowed to land. "Having to stop just short of our destination I'm afraid. Bit of a bind landing up by the old castle what."

Clarence raised a hand, "But we are close though?"

"Oh golly yes. It's just up through the forest there."

Clarence looked out across the woodland. It looked a bit spooky to him and he wasn't too sure if it was such a great idea to go through it, but it seemed the only way and Hogbert was keen. "Is it safe," he said, as they jumped down from the airship.

"Indeed it is. It's the other forest that's haunted, dreadful tree spirits in there… This one is more or less safe," he said as he bumbled forward and pulled on the rucksack.

Clarence pulled a bag over his shoulder too and frowned at what the lord had just said, "More or less?" That meant, to Clarence, that there was a chance of something dreadful happening and he shivered a little at the prospect.

Ace bumped past and winked at the lad, "Hey. Hoggy says it's safe in there. It's gonna be safe right?"

"Hmm. More or less," said Clarence as he cautiously followed the others.

Deep into the forest they went as the density of the trees blocked out a great amount of the suns light, giving the impression of dusk. A howl suddenly echoed through the wood and as the team stopped a call came out from the distance. A man stumbled through the thick darkness of the forest. His face was ashen and as he reached the group they could see his ripped clothes. "You alright buddy?" Said Ace, walking to the man.

He babbled something in French and pointed into the darkness of the woods behind him. His eyes were hollow and seemed soulless as he jabbered on to the group, clearly petrified by something.

"He says something about a dog? A big dog by the sounds of it."

"Oui. Le Loup!" Shouted the man. The howl got louder as the whatever it was neared them. The Frenchman made a funny squeaking noise and ran for his life, disappearing into the bushes as something dark moved before them. It seemed to bounce from tree to tree then it would prowl for a moment in the thicket. Again it bounced up against the side of a great oak and waited for a minute as it watched its prey. Both Ace and Harry pulled their guns and took aim as the creature slid down and began its ground level manoeuvres again. Closer and closer it got until some light beamed through a gap in the trees, revealing the beast to be a very large and rather scary looking wolf-man.

"I say, it's a bloody werewolf," said Hogbert as he fumbled in his bag for something.

"How the heck do we kill it Hoggy?" Growled Ace.

"Kill it? Good gosh no." A large flash followed as Lord Flemington-Ward took a photograph of the creature. "Got ya."

But the monster suddenly snarled and began to run at high speed towards them. Shots whizzed through the forest and past the werewolf as it dodged the bullets with a lightening fast reaction.

"I think it's camera shy," called Hogbert as he

lifted his satchel in front of his face and everyone ducked down.

There was a moment of silence and suddenly… SQUEAK! Standing before the werewolf was the Clown and his squeaky nose held out at arms length. The creature tilted its head and listened intently as the Clown squeezed the nose again. The werewolf crouched down to the ground with its bottom in the air, as if it were about to pounce but this time it had a furiously wagging tail.

"Go fetch it," shouted the Clown and he threw the nose into the thicket. The beast bolted after it with Mr. Fluffles in hot pursuit.

"What the heck was that Clown?" Ace shook his head as he stood. "Did that just happen?" He grabbed Harry's hand and helped her up.

The group began to laugh, out of nervousness or something else but the relief was evident.

"I know dogs and he may be a big, killing machine of a werewolf but at the end of the day, he's still just a cuddly ol' pooch."

The creature scampered back through the bushes with the terrier and spat the nose back out. Clown picked it up and popped it back onto his face. "Woof," he shouted. The werewolf tilted it's head and growled. Clown growled back and for several seconds a strange exchange of growls and whines passed between the two until the creature turned and began to walk slowly through the forest. "We best follow him," said Clown, "He's taking us to the castle, where he lives."

The rest of the journey was short and in a matter of an hour or so they had reached the castle. It stood in the centre of a huge chasm with only a single bridge connecting it to the main land, almost like a tiny island in its own right. The shard of land that housed the castle looked almost too brittle for the building that balanced upon it. The castle itself cast its shadow over the team who had stopped in a state of awe as the werewolf plodded its way up the stone path to the bridge.

"Well I never!" Exclaimed Hogbert as he took out his camera again.

Clown wandered ahead with a brave Mr. Fluffles padding along beside him, "Come on then You lot. No time to waste eh?"

The castle seemed so much bigger as the team reached the front door and as the werewolf pushed the door it creaked open, sending an eerie echo throughout the darkened hall that awaited them. A very grand staircase snaked its way from the darkness and a figure moved down them. It had the impression of floating as it moved and its cloak covered its feet. The group remained silent as the figure appeared in front of them, staring at them with cold grey blue eyes. Suddenly a hand flung out from the cloak and a fanged mouth opened, spilling words in a very stereotypically vampiric accent, "Velcome to castle Von Veedlink. I am the count Dorkus Von Veedlink and you are?" A bony white finger pointed at young Clarence.

"Oh. I'm Clarence, Clarence Bunn sir."

"And vat have you come here for?"

Clarence stood, a little shy now that everyone's eyes were on him to be the spokesman. Ace poked him in the ribs and he jumped, "I… I mean we are here looking for someone and… something."

"You vish to find zee artefact?" He stroked the werewolf's head as he spoke and this unnerved the lad.

"Urm. Well in a sense yes. You see we need to get it before the others do and then we can save Kelly."

"You NEED to find it do you?"

Clarence felt something tremble up his spine, "Yes we do sir. It's because…"

"I do not vish to know you reasonings, but I am aware of zee girl you vish to find." He smiled and this really put Clarence on edge. All the boy could concentrate on were the fangs, and they were real fangs, not like the pretend ones worn by those gothic types in the graveyard. He wondered if the vampire was eyeing him up for his next meal or not. "Please sir. Tell me what you know."

"Come and I vill tell you all I know of ziss…" He turned very suddenly, swooping his cloak theatrically and walked off, beckoning to the group to follow with his long, talon-like fingers, "Come come, my friends. Explore my castle and make yourselves at home. Dinner will be served at five." And with that, he seemed to just vanish into the darkness.

"Oh golly, he was rather frightening wasn't he?" Said Clarence as he turned to the others.

Clown wandered over to a large dresser and opened its doors, revealing several bottles of varying shapes and sizes, "Well he did say to make ourselves at home."

"Ya wanna go explore buddy?" Said Ace as he grabbed the lads arm.

"Have fun boys," laughed Harry as she watched the two of them wander up the staircase. She sat on a large sofa, put her feet up and opened a book, shaking her head with a smile.

The castle was beautiful and gothic and

everything one could expect from a Transylvanian castle in the middle of the mountains. There were bats hanging from the rafters above like drops of black water, waiting to fall at any moment and suits of armour standing lining the hall ways. Clarence trembled a little as floorboards creaked beneath their feet.

"Ain't this a great castle huh? I love Europe for it's history."

"Oh really?" Said Clarence in a most unimpressed tone. He really didn't find castles interesting in any way shape or form and he especially was not enjoying this castle very much either. Maybe it was the dust or the paintings that seemed to follow him with their eyes, or perhaps it was just the shear spookiness of the place and its owner being a blood sucking vampire. "Can we go back down with the others yet?"

"Hey, no way buddy. This is great ain't it?"

Not particularly, thought Clarence as he shuddered at the painting of an eerie looking family with no eyes. "So Ace? Tell me about yourself. I'd love to know about all of your adventures."

Now if there was something Ace loved more than adventuring and flying and generally dangerous shenanigans, it was talking about them and about how great he was, because, he really was actually really rather great. "Well it all started with my pa. He was an inventor back then and used to build engines and this one time he built an engine and put it on wheels and put me on it and, well, he just let it go. Dang, I hadn't ever seen anything like it and from that day I was kinda obsessed with going fast and dangerous."

"So you're father actually put you onto a speeding invention and just watched you zoom off?" Clarence was in shock, the only thing his father had done was shout and get drunk and gamble.

"Yep." Said Ace with a very proud expression on his face, "That man was awesome and made me the man I am today."

"Hmm," said Clarence. He knew the same feeling, his father had made him who he was today but that somebody was nowhere near the kind of man that Ace was. He thought it funny how life did that, how one person could have such an amazing role model and the next person had no role models.

The dinning hall was immense with a table that could seat fifty if required. It was laden with food and drink as if the count had been expecting them and he now sat at the head of the table in his grand chair that sported carvings of skulls, "Please. Eat and drink. You must be… Ravenous." His eyes glinted as he said the word, knowing full well that it would keep his guests wondering. "I feel I already know you, my guests and ve have only just met." He acknowledged Flemington-ward. "Your great uncle? Lord Crisp?"

"Yes. Crispy as we all called him. Did you know him?"

The count nodded, "He vas a regular visitor here at zee castle. You look just like him although I remember him to be much taller."

"He was a tall chap. Dead now though."

"A shame. He may still be alive if he had only taken my offer."

Hogbert raised the monocle to his eye and leaned over the table a little more, "Whatever do you mean old boy?"

The count merely laughed and moved on to the next guest. "Zee Clown. Fascinating attire."

The Clown sat with a bottle of wine in his hand and hiccoughed, "What? Ain't you seen a bloody Clown before?"

"I have, but you. You are different. You have the heart of a lion and a liver of stone."

"Eh?"

Again the count moved on to the next guests, "Zee lovers. I am a passionate man and have a strong connection with you two. How alike you both are and how romantic that you both have felt such pain in love, but now you are interweaved in a complex pattern of emotions." Ace and Harry sat hand in hand and stared at the count as he nodded at them. "I feel something so powerful within you that it can never be broken… Your spirits are fated." He looked at Clarence and the boy stared sheepishly at his host.

"So what can you tell me… I mean us. About what you know." Stuttered the boy.

"I know zat you search for a dead girl. Zis I know because she is of kin to me."

"You know Kelly?" Clarence leaned across the table and grabbed a goblet of what appeared to be a rather thick, red liquid.

"Is zis vat she is known as now? Kelly?…"
Clarence nodded frantically.

"Yes, I have been expecting her for some time. But I fear zere vill be an ending." He twisted the huge green stoned ring on his finger almost nervously, "…But you see. Some things are written and so zey must be."

"What will end Mr. count? Please?"

"I cannot say because I do not know. But I can

tell you zee tale of which you desire."

Clarence continued to nod, making himself look rather simple as the count continued.

"Many years ago a cursed man came to my door. His name vas Lupine and he had with him a much desired object. It was an object that could give life eternal. But zee object was not a solid thing, it vas knowledge. He knew something that could be used in a most arcane ritual. It is frowned upon in our circles but alas, zees fools continue to play with life and death. I could not kill him so I kept him… Quiet!"

Clarence looked at the werewolf, "Is he Lupine?"

"Yes he was. I had to change him. He needed to have zee final artefact locked within him so no other could take it. But now the others come here to take it and I fear they already know zee secret… ingredient."

"Ingredient?"

"Yes Clarence. It is an ingredient for zee ritual. For many years my family has lived here, in zis castle. It has slowly grown around us for a millennia. So many years I have been here. So many faces I have seen pass through. There vas once a time ver our family vould scour zees lands, searching and drinking zee blood of zee lone traveller, or zee drunken villager on his vey home in the dead of night. Vee vere feared back zen by a naïve vorld... But unfortunately, as time vent by the family within have passed by zee hand of humanity. I remain zee last Von Veedlink. Heir to zis ever lasting life of death."

Clarence now spoke in a whispered voice, "You are dead like Kelly?"

The count nodded slowly as he pressed his fingers together, "We are both from zee circle of zee dead. I am but a creature of the night, cursed to death, but she however, has something very unique about her. She is from a very different place."

"Where? You must tell me, I need to know."

"I can not tell you zis, but I can tell you one thing. The spirits of zee dead visit me in my daylight slumber and zey show me things. I have seen that she is becoming like you."

"Uh?"

"Her death becomes life Clarence. Soon she vill be as alive as you and your friends here."

"But they said she was dying?"

The count laughed, "Only her death dies. It is changing, a metamorphosis, that is all." He stood and addressed the table, "Please excuse me lady and gentleman, but I have an errand to run."

Suddenly the main doors burst open and

Doctor Andrew waltzed in with his small group of men, "Don't move. We're here for the artefact." He looked at the count and pointed at him, "You know what I want Von Veedlink."

"Vat is zee meaning of zis? You cannot just valk into my castle and…" But a loud bang echoed around the great hall and the count was blown backwards. The werewolf snarled and looked up to where the blast had come from. Two figures stood at the open window, one held a smoking gun as the other waved his rifle back and forth over the group. "Ello Clawence," called Mr. Chinigan

"Now I have your attention," hissed the doctor, "I suggest you put down you guns and raise your hands."

Ace slammed his guns onto the table and lowered Harry's for her, "Put it down sweet heart. We don't want trouble."

"Well said my American friend. You are outnumbered, outgunned and outwitted." He opened out his arms and Turnbuckle appeared from another door at the other side of the hall with the Mime.

Clarence looked round at the ringmaster, "What? I thought you…"

"For the right price sir, I am anybodies," said Turnbuckle menacingly.

The lad looked back to the Doctor, "Where is she?"

"Oh the dead girl? Here, have her back."

Clarence couldn't believe his eyes. For the first time in so long, there she was, his Kelly. He ran to her as she ran past doctor Andrew. Clarence felt her next to him and time stood still. It was now just the two of them, there in the hall, with no one else around. Her smell, her temperature, it was all so familiar but yet so different. "You're alive," he whispered.

"What do mean Clarence?"

"I mean you're not dying. They lied to you." He stared into her eyes and for the first time he saw a faint glimmer of life. That deathly haze was going and he could almost see her soul. "I've missed you so much." He pulled her close and held her so tight.

"I've missed you too," she paused for a moment, "Clarence? You're hugging me." She pulled away and grabbed his hand, pulling it to her chest. "My heart still has no beat Clarence." She looked at his face. It was so different from their last encounter. He was dirty and rough and his shirt was hanging out, very un-Clarence-like, but very nice she thought. They had both changed so much, with her becoming alive and him, she sniffed and a tear ran down her cheek.

Clarence wiped the drop away with his thumb. "I don't care about your heart not beating Kelly. All I care about is you and I will never lose you again… I love you."

Kelly felt a shot of heat rise up to her face and smiled as she looked at the floor, "I love you too Clarence."

"Very sweet," applauded Doctor Andrew, "But we have no time for this. I have business to attend to." He walked over to the count and placed a small vile next to the gun shot wound, filling it with blood. "The final artefact." He raised his hand to show the room his trophy to much applause from his men. "Bring the girl."

Two men in robes walked out to Kelly, "What about the lad?"

"Bring him too. He may be of use to us… We may need a bargaining chip… or a sacrifice." As they grabbed the couple, Ace shouted out to his friend, "I'll find you buddy… I'll find you."

Together at last

"So how did you do it?" Said Clarence as he stood on the flight deck, staring coldly at the back of his enemy. He wished he could untie his hands and get them around the throat of the man, because at that moment this mild mannered coward had a heart of fire and was very cross.

"Oh Clarence. I do so admire your guile but you see, I need your girl so that I can be ever living."

"But why? What is wrong with being mortal?"

Andrew laughed, "What is wrong he asks? I'll tell you sir. This world has so much to offer and such a rich future for the likes of an immortal. The girl has a foot both in our world and that of the afterlife… Imagine that. Think of the possibilities." He paced with his hands behind his back. "But I need her before she becomes mortal and this is why we must waste not another second."

"And then what?"

"Then the dead girl will become alive for a short period before she dies… for good."

"Damn you," shouted Clarence.

"No Clarence, damn you and damn your dead girl and damn your little friends for scuppering my plans and making this simple ritual so incredibly, bloody, difficult…"

Clarence felt a little warm glow inside, knowing that he had made life hard for the Necromancers, but through his little victory something still bothered him. "How did Turnbuckle know where Kelly was every time? He must be very bright… Brighter than you anyway."

The Doctor burst out into uncontrollable laughter, "Oh my, do you really think that the foolish carnie could have planned this by himself? No, no, no. I've always pulled the strings on my puppets. Every part of this has been by my hand."

Clarence blushed from his back firing insult. "But he… How did…" But his words and reasoning's were lost as the doctor glared at him.

"I planted everything in that fools head. I told him were La Douche would be when he left the mortuary. I had the girls meet with your dead girl and take her to Penny's Den." He laughed once more and turned back to the window. "You seem to forget that the Necromancers have been around for many many years, slipping into governments and politicians. Winding our tendrils around the throats of leaders and taking over everything." His eyes burned with an evil passion that scared Clarence. "We shall be in Mexico soon and just in time for the day of the dead." He rocked on his heels, admiring the view and still not looking at the lad. "Take him away."

A large, robed man pulled Clarence away, but the lad didn't struggle. He had his girl back and that was all that mattered for the time being.

The door burst open and Clarence fell in. "Hi," he managed as he stumbled to the floor.

Kelly grabbed him and helped him to his feet, "Are you alright?" She said, "Did they hurt you?"

"No. But even if they had have done, I wouldn't have cared." Kelly untied his hand and he sat down on the bed, "You know they want to take your death from you?"

"Yes, I guessed that was what they had planned." She looked so sad as she stared at the floor. But Clarence put a reassuring arm around her. "It saddens me that we have had all this time apart and now the time we have is to be so limited."

Kelly looked at him with her glazed, dead eyes and smiled as she placed a hand on her chest, "But absence had made this heart grow fonder."

As they stared into each others eyes Clarence

suddenly remembered and he reached a hand into his waistcoat pocket, "I have something for you." He pulled the ring out and placed it on the girls finger. "I want you to have this because it's a sign of my devotion to you."

"But I can't take this Clarence. However much I want to, and I really do, I just can't."

The lads heart sank, "But you said… I thought… But why?"

"Because our lives are so different. Soon I shall be gone and this body will be no more and this ring…" She stared at it. It was ancient and beautiful and it sparkled like a star in the candlelight. "… will be lost."

"But as long as you have it now you will know how much I love you."

Kelly began to cry. Her new tears were not being wasted and she grabbed Clarence and held him tightly, "Then I shall love to wear it for you Clarence," she managed through a haze of new tears, "For as long as I am on this earth."

Clarence seized the moment, now was as good a time as any other he thought. "Then where will you go?" There he thought, I've asked the question. She must know the answer to such a thing, she was dead after all.

"I'll go back to my father."

"Your father?" Clarence began to think of all

the times he had been dragged to church by the Wilkomsir family and the time he had spent wondering just who 'our father' really was. The problem was, the boy thought too much, or so Mr. Wilkomsir had frequently told him. His mind was really rather scientific and it needed the hard facts, but now he was thinking that he should have perhaps paid a little more attention to the prayers on a Sunday morning instead of staring out of the window at the pigeons and how he could embalm them. "As in…?" He gestured to the sky.

Kelly giggled, "Do you mean the gods?"

Clarence deflated and relaxed, "Yes, that's who I meant."

"No. I mean my father. My dad… Death." She blinked and looked so very matter of fact after she had said that word.

"What as in, DEATH?"

Kelly laughed and pushed him in the shoulder, "Yes him."

Well that explains a lot, thought Clarence, "Don't you think he might be a little, well, you know, cross?"

"Oh he is always cross. It is his job to be solemn but that's why I left."

"So you just left… where?"

Kelly huffed, "Please Clarence, why do you

need to know these things? I want to talk about us and just be with you tonight."

Clarence knew right then that a dramatic subject change was in order and he took her hand, kissing the girls cold, pale fingers, "Close your eyes Kelly." And she did, and he knew exactly what to do as he leaned in towards her.

The morning came as the South American sun burned across a dry and very different landscape to what the rather English Clarence was used to. He had barely slept all night, talking to Kelly about everything and anything, about life and death and them, but taking special care not to mention 'you know who'. His bleary eyes gazed out across deserts with their strange spiky plants and trees and he wondered how anyone could live in such a place. But there on the horizon was a town, right in the middle of nowhere, which is in fact what the town was called, Nowhere. The name just summed up the town perfectly, for as far as the eye could see in every direction was lifeless desert and cacti, but for the mountains on the horizon. The town itself however, was bustling with life and colour as the townsfolk prepared for the Dia de muertos, or the day of the dead. Everything was being covered in floral garlands as wooden skeletons sat on chairs and in windows with hats and clothing on. The group walked through the people towards the boarding house, lead by the Doctor. He carried a long bag and a large backpack and stared ahead as if in a trance as he walked.

Kelly ran her hand over one of the wooden effigies and giggled, "Catrina." She said, "My mother."

"Uh?" Said Clarence. He hadn't wanted to ask about whether there was a mother after last night, but as Kelly had brought it up, he thought it to be a safe opportunity.

"I didn't know you had a mother… I mean I guessed you must have but…" Clarence had got to the point in conversation where he wasn't sure what to say next and where he hoped and prayed that his bumbled sentence would be completed by the other person, this was one of those lucky occasions as Kelly interrupted.

"It's not like it is here Clarence. I wasn't born or anything, I kind of just happened. My mother and father are just figures in my life… death, that I call parents." She held his hand, "This body was just something I stepped into."

"How could you just step into a body? I mean… I'm sorry to ask but you have made me curious now."

"I made this shell. My true self is more of a

spiritual form."

"Like a soul?"

"More or less. If that's the label you want to give it but for me it is what I am and have always been."

Clarence worried for a moment and then asked, "So what do you look like? I mean, what do you really look like?"

Kelly laughed, "I look like this but a little more…" She pondered on this for a second, "See through," she winked and Clarence blushed.

"Wow," he said.

Messy in Mexico
The saloon was filled with decorations and a happy looking barman stood behind the bar cleaning a glass. He nodded once to Andrew, "Welcome to Nowhere," he said before spitting into the glass and carrying on polishing.

The Doctor stopped and turned to face Clarence, "The town is yours to explore but trust me, if you try to escape then Mr. Chinigan and Mr. Boil here will not hesitate in killing you without a question. Do you understand?"

The lad nodded and said nothing. He was terrified of the two assassins and since Chinigan had said he would kill Clarence anyway, he was more afraid than ever. He squeezed Kelly's hand and felt himself recoiling slightly behind the girl. What kind of man did that he thought, it sickened him to the very core at how cowardly he was and he knew everyone could see it too. It was as if he was a natural target to anyone who wanted a go. He wasn't sure what made him stand out so much, perhaps it was the fact that he didn't really stand out at all that made him so obviously outstanding to every bully and ruffian out there. A tiny flashback appeared in his head and Clarence began to relive all of those moments where he had been targeted by people in his life. School was relatively easy to work out as it was always somebody's job to be bullied and rather unfortunately for Clarence it had been his job, from day one if he looked back hard enough he had been that person. He remembered that horrid boy David Witherington who had made the class laugh and who had been so popular for his mistreatment of the other, not so popular children. He wondered what had ever happened to that boy who had been so cruel to him and hoped he was in a grotty prison somewhere for being horrid, or the evil side to Clarence hoped he had got on the wrong side of the wrong person and fallen foul of a blade or club. But deep down he knew that the child he had once feared was now probably a wealthy lawyer of something, with two children, a beautiful wife and a Labrador retriever. Clarence had often wondered how the teasing of others could bring such joy but had once laughed at another unfortunate as he was picked on, perhaps it had been the lore of the playground to run with the bully or face harassment. Those days, were days that he could quite easily wipe from his mind and never have back. If only he had had someone like Ace back then. Perhaps life would've been a whole lot different, or maybe Ace had been a bully? Or maybe he and Ace would have bullied people together. He shuddered at the thought and something else popped into Clarence's thought process as it quite often did, what if Kelly had been at the school? What if she had seen the weak and worthless boy in short trousers whose father had lost him in a game of poker, what then? Would she still love him now? He tried desperately to cleanse his mind of that thought, it wasn't nice and it hurt when he thought about it. And then from school, he had left behind all those bullies and a brave new world awaited for the lad? No, it was almost as bad with the local lads leering and joking about the skinny, adopted boy who lived in the morgue. They would point and laugh at him and even the adults in the area would whisper about that Bunn boy and about how strange they thought he was. Then he had met Kelly and things got better but she was taken and he lost his confidence again to the assassins known as Chinigan and Boil. They were like the bullies from his childhood, in fact he was in no doubt that they had most definitely been the type to beat up the lonely child in the playground as everyone else laughed. He looked at his Kelly and at how beautiful she was, in a dead kind of way and then he looked at how ugly the assassins were. Such contrast in people he thought.

"Right," called Doctor Andrew, "Boil with the girl. Chinigan with the boy."

Chinigan grinned his black toothed grin as he played with his knife, "This will be fun eh, Clawence?"

The lad shuddered at the thought of his every move being watched by the hideous men and wished for a back bone.

The couple tried desperately to pretend they were not being followed, but it was difficult and by now the town was almost in its full flow of celebrations.

"Can you feel it Clarence?" Said Kelly as they wandered into a market and past people with their faces painted like skulls, "I can feel the death all around us. It feels amazing. I wish you could feel the spirits too."

But the lad wasn't too sure himself about the joy and excitement of death, "Do you know why they do this Kelly? I mean it's all well and good having celebrations about things, but death? Really?"

Kelly stopped and held her mans hands tightly, "When I go…" Clarence tried to interrupt but Kelly stopped him and she started again, "When I go, will you celebrate my life?"

"I'll morn for you forever." He felt himself welling up as he thought about the inevitable.

"That's not what I asked. Will you celebrate the days we spent together? Will you think of me always? Will the time we had together be worth your happy thoughts?"

"Of course I will." He could feel tears blurring his vision.

"That's why they celebrate Dia de muertos. They are celebrating those who have passed over and they rejoice because one day they will join their loved ones in a better place."

"Do you mean heaven? Is there such a place. You must know, you must've been there and…" He paused, "…will you be there, waiting for me?"

Tears filled Kelly's eyes too as she looked up at him, "Heaven is whatever you want it to be and when or where you want. If you believe then it will be." She put a finger onto his chest, "I will always be just here Clarence, for as long as you want me to be, I'll be there, just inside." A blink pushed free a tear on either cheek, "And as for me visiting heaven. This is heaven for me Clarence, being with you is my heaven." Kelly rested her head onto his chest, she could hear his heart pounding beneath his coat and longed for her own heart to beat with his, just once. She knew that tonight, the ritual would take place and she would lose her death but gain life for a moment and that would be the time she longed for. She would embrace Clarence and die in his arms for the final time her body would turn to dust and she would be back with her father and Clarence would be alone. She prayed that it would be like that and that Clarence would go back home, but something inside told another story. She saw the true horror of it all in a vision of her own future and it chilled her to the very core. That she would be taken and Doctor Andrew would become immortal and then have Clarence killed like a lamb as he cried for her. She closed her eyes and pushed her head closer to him.

Andrew stood on a cliff edge with the staff of Mahooganooba clutched in his hands. His crimson robe flapped in the hot breeze that swept up from the canyon below like an oven door opening. The canyon was known as the death hole of Nowhere, so named due it being a place of a mass sacrifice about a hundred years previously. The town had not been built at that time but as it grew, the townsfolk would say that many ghosts and spirits would visit from the canyon. It was a sacred but scary place that no one ever ventured near and some even said that death himself lived in a hole down there. The doctor grinned, the perfect place for a Necromancers ritual he thought as he gazed at the setting sun and breathed in the air. It smelt of warm dust and death. He played with the tiny vial in his pocket and smirked at how wickedly clever he was. The dawning of Dia de muertos would soon be upon them and he would have all power, as well as death of course. A noise made him turn and he saw his men building a temporary alter of sacrifice. It was beautiful and he walked to it, noticing the writings around its outside, the cryptic scribblings from an era so far back that the civilisation who wrote it were long past and diluted into the new world. "Send for the girl," he snarled.

"And Bunn ya lordshipness? What of the boy." Said a small man with a west country accent and a rather ill fitting toupee.

"Have Chinigan kill him. And tell him not to bugger it up or he'll be next."

The town was reaching fever pitch as the sun disappeared and lanterns were lit all around the place. Clarence noticed a small man run through the crowd and bump into Chinigan. He felt nauseous as if a knowing sickness of the impending horror about to take place. Chinigan nodded and eyeballed the lad with a sickening snarl that made the hairs stick up on Clarences neck. Suddenly Boil grabbed Kelly and began to pull her away, she screamed and Clarence moved forward to defend the girl, but as he did so a large fist slammed into his head making the world spin. The crowd blurred and skeletal faces moved in curious shapes as he spun in a circle. He saw Chinigan and the glint of a blade in the man's hand as he focused. The assassin moved closer and looked twisted in his expression like a monster. He glanced to where Kelly had been but the crowds had swallowed them up like the sea taking down a dead bird. Why had no one stopped her from being taken? Why had they let him get punched in the face? Again he looked back at his would be killer, his eye was now already starting to swell and he had almost lost the vision to the blood forming in his soft tissues around his eye. Chinigan was closer now and he could almost smell the smell of rancid smoke on the man's clothing. A firecracker went off and lots of cheers filled his ears and it hurt his brain, or it may have been his eye that hurt, but whichever it had been it was not going to conceal the pain he was about to experience. Chinigan roared as he pulled back an arm, ready to thrust the knife into the helpless Clarence. He stood and waited for his imminent death to come as time slowed to an almost paused rate, but then something clicked in the young man's head, something that had been locked away for so many years and had now only just surfaced for the first time like a new born to the absolute realisation of life. Clarence was not going to die today, he just absolutely was not going to be murdered by this scruffy man before him and he ran for his life, through the crowd like a rabbit would run through its burrows. His slight frame allowed him to slip through the people as the big, clumsy Chinigan barged and waded, gaining nothing but harsh looks and resentment.

Clarence panted as he stopped in a doorway, he wanted to be sick but thought how unkind that would be for the owner. He had to find Kelly and save her and if that meant him being killed in the process then so be it, he didn't care, just as long as he stopped the ritual and saved her death from its impending life. The towns clock chimed ten and the crowed went a little madder than it already was with more firecrackers popping and fireworks whizzing through the air and into the sky, lighting the tops of the buildings and illuminating the wooden, skeletal statues that stood around the roofs like an army of the undead, about to attack. Two hours thought Clarence, I only have two hours to save her, as he regained his breath and stood tall. Two hours to find out where the ritual was going to take place. He turned and looked in through the door and was almost knocked back by his coincidental stop outside the towns' morgue and Undertakers. "Hmm." Said Clarence and he opened the door.

A ping filled the empty waiting area and Clarence noticed the smell straight away, it was the smell that had filled his nostrils since he was five, the smell of the embalming fluid, the smell of blood, the smell of death.

"Ello." Came a voice as a very round man appeared from the back, he wiped his hands across his apron, leaving a trail of some unknown liquid and held out an opened palm. Clarence shook the sticky hand, "Hello," he said back to the man.

"You Englishman man?"

Clarence nodded, "Yes. I am from England," he said.

"I love England man. I never been there but I love it man." He laughed and reached over the counter to land a slap on Clarence's arm.

"Oh? Well I'm a Morticians ass…"

But the Mexican interrupted, "I just knew it man. I could tell as soon as you walked in I thought, this man's a Mortician man…" His voice seemed to get louder as he spoke but before it reached its deafening crescendo, the Mexican Mortician turned his volume back down to a normal volume, "I am Sanchez."

"Well hello Sanchez, my names Clarence."

The man's round face beamed, "I love that name! It's so English man." Shouted Sanchez. "We got boring names here man, but you English, you got the best names!"

"Golly," thought Clarence, as he remembered a previous conversation with Ace.

"So what happened to your eye man? Did someone hit you or something? Was it the hustle and bustle out there?" The Mexican did a little wiggling dance before carrying on. "It happened to my little boy Juan once, he got a broken arm but HEY, it's time for celebration eh?."

"Well actually, a bloody assassin did it. He's chasing me right now."

Sanchez shook his head, "Bastardo. Who paid this assassin man?"

Clarence was feeling a little uneasy, but something was very likeable about the big round Mexican, and although Sanchez' excited tone was a little irritating to Clarence's aching head he decided to spill the beans and tell him, "Necromancers."

Sanchez went a little cross eyed and his cheeks puffed out which in turn caused his moustache to stick out to the sides like the handle bars of a bike, "I hate them!" He shouted, "They come here and use the spirits for bad things. I'd kill them if I had the chance man. They use my ancestors' souls for their dirty magic and that ain't right man. They got no respect for the dead."

"You're absolutely right Mr. Sanchez, but…" The ping of the door made both men look up to see an extremely cross looking Chinigan bursting in with his knife in hand.

"No escape Clawence, not this time. I'm gonna to bloody skin you alive you little ratbag."

Clarence pressed himself up against the counter and trembled like a leaf as the man closed in, "You're not running away this time."

Suddenly there was a click behind Clarence as a shotgun barrel appeared and rested on the boy's shoulder followed by the booming voice of Sanchez past his ear, "Drop your weapon or I kill you grubby assassin man."

Chinigan snarled, "You won't bloody shoot me fatty."

Sanchez laughed, "You're right, I won't shoot. But my boys will kick your ass… Boys!" Suddenly, three very big men stormed in from the back, with their heavy leather aprons on, each carrying an item of Morticians equipment, which mainly consisted of the sharp or knobbly variety. "This man is one of those Necromancers man."

There was a tinkling noise as Chinigans little knife fell to the floor, "Oh bugger," he whispers as the three men grabbed him and dragged him out the back.

"What will they do to him?" Said Clarence as he stared, shocked at what had just taken place.

"Oh they will rough him up, not a little, probably a lot man. Just like he deserves for threatening their pops eh?" Sanchez laughed again and but the gun back under the counter, "The gun was empty anyway man." He laughed and then produced a bottle of some rather turbid looking liquid, "But this is full man, and it's gonna be the only shots gonna be fired in here today man."

"But I need to go and find Kelly before…"

"You don't wanna insult old Sanchez do you man?"

Clarence thought about what had just

happened and shook his head quickly as he held out a hand, taking the small glass and sniffing its contents. He had never experienced such a smell before, not even when rotting corpses had been brought into the Mortuary, and in actual fact they smelt a little less nostril scratching than the almost glowing liquor in his hand.

"Screw Dutch courage man, this is Mexican courage." He sunk the liquid and breathed deeply through his nose and nodded at Clarence. "Your turn man, take the shot buddy."

Clarence held his nose, "Chin chin," he said as he poured the drink into his mouth. It felt like fire as it hit his tongue and seemed to grow claws as it rasped its way down his throat. "Golly." Croaked Clarence. "Now where's this ritual?" He squeaked.

"You drink like a Mexican man. Now you wanna go to the edge of town and you will see the lights on the hill. I guess that's where it will be. That's the usual place they go. Nobody goes there no more though man. The place is evil but I guess you gotta do what you gotta do eh?"

Clarence nodded slowly. He could still feel the drink inside him and as it tried to burn its way out from his body like a furnace. "Thanks," tried

Clarence as his voice now seemed to have vanished and he wondered if it would ever come back again.

"You come back soon English." Sanchez raised the bottle with a mischievous grin, "We finish this eh man?"

"We will. Thank you." Wheezed Clarence, leaving the building and hitting the crowd once more.

The mysterious liquid fizzed in the lad's gut and he could feel it warming him from the inside with a fresh and rather enjoyably fuzzy feeling that rushed through this body like lava in his blood. He looked round to wave at Sanchez but the building no longer existed, instead there stood an abandoned shack. Clarence frowned but put it down to the bizarre feeling he now had in his head as he pushed through the mass of people with a new fire within in his soul. The Mexican courage was certainly living up to its name and as he caught the first glimpse of the hill top, Clarence felt a strange energy that pushed him harder and faster to his destination. The edge of the town came and went, and now it was just a winding pathway with a slight incline to the top of the hill. Another bell chimed, eleven o'clock and the townsfolk erupted into hysteria. It would soon be midnight and the new dawn, the dawn of the day of the dead and a new era for the treacherous Doctor Andrew. Clarence stomped up the hill and with every step he felt more and more cross. Something drove him from inside like an internal steam engine that puffed and chugged, filling his muscles with an energy that appeared from nowhere. He didn't even need to take hold of the crooked fence that led up the track for the weary traveller, he was working on pure Bunn power and it felt good as he marched with a fury in heart and liquor in his blood . He had had his girl taken once before, but not again, not this Clarence, for this Clarence was a new and improved and enraged and in love Clarence with the fire of Mexico in his belly and the nerves of a man on the edge of his tether. He thought about his friends, if only they were here to see this, Ace would pat his shoulder and Harry would kiss his cheek and the Clown would probably and undoubtedly raise a bottle or five before passing out or vomiting. If only he had always believed this much in himself, then perhaps he would be a different man all together, maybe this scrawny young thing would have been something else, like a man of notability around town. But no, he was Clarence Poggy-Bobbins Bunn, and he was proud to be who he was.

As he neared the summit he gritted his teeth and thought about the words he would say. Maybe he would rush in with a furious passion and fight the lot of them, but then fisticuffs had never been his way, in fact he had never been in a fight in his life, so his next idea was to just stand there and point and wave a finger and look manly about it, yes, that was it, manly. He could hear Andrew mumbling away in a strange foreign language, the ritual must be under way he thought and with that he gained speed.

Andrew stood with his arms out to the sides, the staff of Mahooganooba in one hand and the vial in the other. "Oh spirits of the dead. Oh great spirits. Come to this world and take this offering that I bring to you on this, the eve of Dia de muertos." Hear me great ancestors and be afraid for I have this," he raised the staff above his head, "The Staff of Mahooganooba." And he slammed its base into the dry, red earth at his feet, bringing with it a rumble from the skies. Andrew turned to look out across the canyon and to the peculiar looking clouds that were forming in the distance with lightening flickering within as they moved quickly towards the hill top. "Oh spirits. Come to me and behold the blood of the immortal." He held up the vial of vampires blood and a crack of thunder rumbled across the land, making the ground beneath them shake as if it were beneath the desert itself. He glanced at his pocket watch, it was half past eleven. He smiled and closed his eyes and began to speak in the strange tongue again.

"You will never get away with this you… you horrid man." Shouted Kelly as she tried to struggle free of the hooded men that held her, a gust of hot wind blowing the girls hair over her face.

Doctor Andrew didn't turn to look at the girl as he spoke, "Oh I already have you silly girl. The time is nearly upon us and you will soon be nothing but a pile of dust. I know your secrets you see, the spirits told me."

"Oh really? What is my secret then?" Spat Kelly.

"You have been sent by the great ancestors as my chalice. You hold the death that I so desire. They sent you, admit it"

Kelly laughed at the man, "You have no idea do you? I actually came here to see how you live. To be among the living and to live as one of you. But I was kidnapped and now I am becoming alive… like you."

There was a moment of uncomfortable silence

before Doctor Andrew spoke again, "Well… In that case I have just been really rather lucky haven't I?" He snarled, "Anyway. You know I told Chinigan to kill your Clarence? I told him to make it slow and painful and I imagine he is still dying."

Tears poured from Kelly's eyes as she pulled harder against her captors, "No, no it's not true."

"Oh but it is true dead girl. I bet your little Clarence is dying as we speak. He will not save you now."

And with that, Clarence made the most perfect entrance a man could ever make, in fact it was so perfect a moment that Clarence beamed with delight as he strolled into the clearing and announced to the Necromancers. It was almost as if it had been scripted by whatever gods were on his side at that time. "That's where you're wrong Doctor!"

The whole camp gasped in unison before falling into complete, startled silence, all but Kelly as she called out to him in a mixture of tears and laughter.

"Let her go at once you…" Clarence thought very hard about his next word, but nothing appropriate came to mind, so he just settled with, "Bugger."

The look on the Doctors face was priceless and if Clarence could have taken a picture of it there and then, then he would have done so and he would have kept it in a frame on his wall and would have referred to it as the day that he had been really, rather, bloody amazing, or maybe even the day that that he had foiled the plans of a massive, undercover agency, or even both he mused.

"Ah well you are too late Bunn," shouted the Doctor, interrupting Clarence's self praise, "Can you not see the clouds of death as they gather around us? Can you not feel the Grim Reaper behind you?"

Clarence looked at Kelly with an inkling of fear in his expression, and the worry that maybe death was, literally, right behind him, but she smiled and shook her head, "There is no Grim Reaper here, there is only…" Again Clarence fought for the right words as he walked through the stunned group. His mind raced with words and phrases but nothing surfaced, it was like a boggy marsh of sentences with nothing but confusing confabulations bobbing about like fish heads of nonsense. If only he had rehearsed the dialogue in his head, but then words had never really been the boy's strong point and it was only recently that he had stopped stammering at the slightest sign of any sort of confrontation, which sadly included even the simplest of conversation in Clarences mind. Damn it he thought as he approached the Doctor, come on and think. But then something amazing happened, something that Clarence could never had planned or anticipated in a hundred years, and something that matched his entrance so complimentary that he wondered if he may be dreaming. He pointed over the Doctor's shoulder and boomed, "My friends."

The Slipstream rose up from the canyon like the moon rising out from a dark horizon. It flew over head and bumped into a small group of Necromancers who were standing in a huddle around the sacrificial alter, knocking them down the hill into some awaiting bushes which looked rather spiky and very painful. Ace and Harry jumped down, guns firing into the air for effect and boots kicking into the hooded minions. Clown leaped down too for some action and so too did a very snarly and aggressive Mr. Fluffles. "We're here Christian." Shouted the Clown as he pushed another Necromancer to the ground and stood on him with his standard issue, oversized, clown shoes.

"Ha! It's too late." Called Andrew, as the sound of the bells began to chime from the town, telling that the new dawn had began. He pushed past Clarence, poking him in his good eye and grabbed Kelly from the two men. The clouds moved in a circle above now like the beginnings of a tornado and the Doctor ran to the edge of the cliff and boomed out his best evil villain laugh. "There is nothing can be done fools. I laugh at your futile attempts to save the girl, but she is mine for the taking." He pulled her to him and popped the top from the vial with his thumb, drinking its contents in one. At that moment, a bolt of lightning hit the staff and an ominous green, glowing orb enveloped both the Doctor and Kelly. Clarence staggered forward with a blurry vision and pointed at the pair, "I'll not let you do it you sod," he slurred and with that he ran at his full pace towards them. Everything moved in slow motion as Clarence hurdled over Necromancers and then, as the sky rumbled again, ready for another shock of lightening to complete the ritual, the boy jumped, "NOOOO!" He yelled. The doctor stared, Kelly stared and Clarence landed, perfectly with both hands on the staff. A shudder shot through his body as time sped up to normal speed again as volts of electricity surged through him.

"You've broken the circuit… You idiot. You've

ruined everything."

Clarence smiled at the Doctor as his hair fizzed and smoked. "Give me the staff you cad."

"Ha. Never." The pair pushed and pulled at one another like a couple of toddlers, fighting over a toy.

"I said… give… it… to… me!" Clarence pulled and freed the staff from Andrew's hands. "Oh golly," giggled Clarence as he stared at the Staff in complete disbelief.

Kelly clapped, "Oh well done Clarence."

But Doctor Andrew snarled, "Well, if I can't have her then," he turned and pushed the girl from the cliff, "No one can."

Clarence felt every cell in his body suddenly explode at that point as the Mexican courage took its second wind from his adrenaline and pulled its red fog of rage over his eyes like a blanket, turning him into some kind of puffy eyed, skinny bodied, anger monster. He ran again, but this time he roared like a Spartan warrior into battle, slamming into his enemy like a rhino and knocking them both from the ledge. As they fell through the warm air, Clarence cared not about his impending death because everything that he held dear to him was gone. His friends would morn him fair enough and

they would be sad for a while, but they would be able to continue with their lives with the happy memory of knowing him as a hero, but he could never continue, not without her in his life. And with tears flowing from his stinging eyes he saw something on the cliff face waving frantically at him, it was Kelly, she was still alive, well sort of.
And as Clarence tried to wave back he became aware that his plan had taken on the shape of a very very bad pear, and he said "Bugger."

…And the ground broke his fall as the world went THUD!

Well this is death then!
A tepid breeze blew into Clarence's face, waking him from his deathly slumber. His eyes blinked open but this time with no sting and no pain. "What on earth?" He said as he slowly got to his feet. He was on a beach but the pebbles were not like any beach he had ever seen before. They were black and shone like a billion onyx stones, clustered before him for as far as he could see in both directions. Looking down he noticed his lack of shoes, but the stones didn't hurt his feet, in fact, on the contrary, they felt as soft as sand, which he decided was rather odd. Another thing that unsettled Clarence as he scanned this new and alien environment was the sea, with its almost white appearance, moving as if in reverse with its waves lapping backwards, away from the black beach. Clarence rotated on the spot, but now behind him was a sheer cliff edge, not unlike the one he had just fallen from, but this one was jagged and grey and went up for what seemed like an eternity, up into a grey, almost negative photo looking sky.

"Welcome to limbo Clarence Bunn."

The lad turned with a start to see a man, his black suit was that of an undertaker and he too had a distinct lack of footwear. "Are you?" But before he could finish, the man answered the unasked question.

"Yes. I am death."

"OH. So you're?"

Again, death answered before the question was asked, "Yes. Kelly is my daughter and yes, you are dead Clarence Bunn."

"But I thought you would be…"

"A skeleton in a black robe? No, I am here in a form you would be more comfortable with."

"An undertaker?"

"Does this form not represent anything about your previous life?"

"Well yes, it does but…"

"You expected the robe and skeleton didn't you? Why do you people always prefer the skeleton?" Said death, with a disappointed tone.

"I don't know, it's just…"

"More traditional, I know. How's about this?" Death raised his arms and from behind him a misty swirl began to appear like a sideways tornado. Clarence stepped back a little and watched as a shape in the distance became bigger and bigger until he could see the shape of six horses pulling a chariot. It drew closer and appeared to increase its speed and as it blasted through the air only feet from the young man, the sound of screaming Valkyries filled the air! Clarence ducked and followed the chariot with his eyes as it took a sharp vertical change in its direction up the face of the cliff, up, up until it vanished into the grey clouds above.

"What on earth?" Stammered Clarence.

"Valkyries my dear boy," said the Grimm figure as he watched the sky folding back to its reversing flatness.

"But why…"

"Because it's another form or death" Interrupted death.

Another figure appeared next to Death, it was a women with a beautifully painted skull on her face. "Or this perhaps?"

Someone tapped Clarence on the shoulder and as he turned he was faced with very large blue man dressed in gold and standing on very large and very grumpy looking water buffalo.

"Perhaps Yama is more to your liking."

"No no it's fine thank you," said Clarence as he backed away from the Hindu god of death.

"I knew you would say that!" Said death.

Clarence folded his arms and looked a little cross. "Look. I know you're death and all but, well, could you please not answer my questions before I have finished asking them."

"But it saves time and…" He saw that Clarence was still unimpressed, "But I shall do as you have asked as I value your opinion."

"Thank you."

"You are welcome. So what do you wish to know before I send your soul to which ever place it is that you wish to go?"

"I'd like to see Kelly again if I may."

Death looked under a furrowed brow, "Very well. She is behind you."

Clarence turned and sure enough, there she was, "Kelly!" He yelled as he moved forward to hug the girl, but as he did so, his arms went straight through her. "Oh. You must be."

Kelly nodded, "Yes Clarence, I am in my true form."

"But I saw you on the cliff edge, you were alive."

"And I still am Clarence, but everything has stopped. All that happens in this world is as fast as light, only catching up on itself to reverse again."

Clarence looked over at the sea and sure enough it was now splashing as the sea should, "But what about me?"

Kelly shook her head, "I'm sorry Clarence. You're now rather dead."

"But that's not fair. I mean after all I went

through to save you and now this. I won't be dead, I just will not." He folded his arms in protest and Kelly giggled at him.

"Oh Clarence. You do look funny when you're cross."

He remained expressionless with his bottom lip out in full sulk.

"But I do agree with you. It really isn't fair." She looked at her father, "Father?"

"The answer is no. I cannot take him back. He is dead and that is final," said Death, now also crossing his arms in protest.

"But he did so much for me. He travelled half way across the world and back just for me and besides, I love him."

Death continued to stare with a mournfully bad tempered look on his face. "Oh very well Kelly. But you must understand that it will not just be my decision now. It is taken from my hand." He frowned, "And think of the bloody paperwork too."

Kelly ran through Clarence and hugged her father, "Oh thank you so much."

Clarence stared at them and wished he could have had a father to embrace like that, but the only contact he had ever received was a slap about the head. Perhaps things would have been different if his mother had survived giving birth to him and then maybe his father would not have blamed him for her death and found his comfort in the bottom of a bottle. That was all Clarence had of his father, the memories of a harsh and sad man, memories that poisoned his mind and would wake him in the middle of the night screaming for his mother. There had been a photograph of her on the mantle and he could still see it whenever he closed his eyes, she was beautiful and smiled down at him every day for three years, but then he was taken away and everything changed. But not for the better or worse, because who could say which they would rather have, an abusive father or an abusive foster family? No one cared about what a little boy had to say. No one hugged him or showed him any affection but that was all he had ever really wanted, to be loved.

Kelly turned, "Are you ready Clarence?"

"Ready? For what?"

Deaths voice bellowed, with an echo that made the black pebbles rattle beneath them like an earthquake. "Judgement."

"I'm not sure about that, I mean what will it entail?"

"Judgement is judgement Clarence Bunn."

"Uh huh?" Said Clarence.

"Are you ready boy."
"Well I guess so yes."
 And with that, death raised his arms and said, "Then let judgement commence."
Kelly waved frantically at the young man as a cloud of black enveloped him.
 Clarence gulped as a slow darkness came once more. It was a funny kind of darkness he thought, not like night time darkness, but more of a deep underground cave kind of darkness, the type of darkness that hurt one's eyes from their need to find light. But then something strange happened and it felt apparent that he was no longer standing on those black, onyx pebbles, but floating in the cold darkness of a starless and airless space. He could hear something in the distance, a hubbub of many people, getting louder and louder and closer as he hung in the air like a Clarence shaped ballon. Something tapped against the bottoms of his feet as he appeared to land, but now he had shoes on and looking down he could make out the shine of fancy, black leather shoes upon an elaborately tiled green floor as the darkness turned to light. They were not his shoes and these clothes, this suit was certainly not his either. He had never owned a suit and even if he have done it certainly wouldn't have

been such a formally pinstriped outfit as this one.

Clarence looked up slowly as the noise got louder and he could see a long room before him, flanked at its left and right by rows upon rows of benches that went up like steps as far as he could focus. "What in the…?" And as his vision cleared and his eyes adjusted to the light he could see the people on the benches, hundreds of them, old men with black suits and white wigs like judges, all mumbling and fussing and coughing with dust falling from their ancient shoulders. There was sudden whoosh of air and light as Clarence now found himself before a huge desk.

"ORDER!" Boomed a voice that belonged to the very large man sitting before him in a large red leather chair. He peered over his little glasses and puffed out his cheeks as a bead of sweat ran down his red forehead, dripping onto the stack of dried and yellowed papers that filled the desk before him. "Name?"

Clarence stood, staring at the man.

"Are you deaf boy, I said NAME?"

"Clarence sir, Clarence Bunn." He felt his voice stammering again, as it always had done in tricky situations. He could feel his nerves shredding as his gut twisted with fear.

Another mumble echoed around the vast room of elderly men.

"ORDER!" Boomed the man again, "You are here today for?" He rustled with some papers and then found the article he wanted. Holding the page up to his eyes the old man looked over it at the boy. "You do not wish to be dead?"

The hubbub got very loud and scrunched up pieces of paper were thrown at Clarence by several disgruntled observers.

"Is this correct boy?" Whined the large, sweating judge.

"That is right sir. I wish to return to life and to be with…"

"SILENCE!"

Clarence looked at the floor in absolute terror. What on earth was going on he thought, but then maybe not even on earth, he shuddered at that thought and continued to look at the floor like a naughty school boy.

"We are the adjudicators. We have been for an eternity and will be for the rest of eternity and forever thereafter. We pass the final judgement on those who do not believe they should be…Dead." There was something in the way he said the word dead, something that chilled the lads very blood. The word seemed to roll from the mans tongue, accentuating every letter in a morbidly seductive manner that made Clarence feel a little nauseous. He had spent most of his life with the dead and around death but this unnerved him in a very creepy manner indeed.

The din erupted again but the man merely stared at the boy over his tiny glasses, "And those who wish to not be dead must have a very valid reason for this. Do YOU have a valid reason for this Clarence Bunn? Do YOU believe that death should be wavered for you to return back to life?" He drummed his fingers impatiently on the desk and not giving the poor boy time to answer he shouted, "WELL?"

"I… I do believe so sir yes."

The adjudicator looked on with a strained expression, "You will have to speak up boy. Our learned colleagues of the court did not hear your plea." His voice was full of sarcasm as he spoke, pushing an uncomfortable and patronising tone at Clarence as his big red jowls wobbled.

"I said I do believe so sir yes."

Suddenly the fat man stood from his desk and walked off.

Clarence's jaw dropped, "But I haven't finished…" He whispered.

Another, skinnier and decidedly older man

hobbled up to the chair, "Order!" He called in a much more shrill voice as he placed a long wig upon his head and pointed at the boy. "So? You wish to return to the place from whence you came? You wish to be alive and wish to NOT be dead?" The mumbling continued and a paper cup bounced across the floor in the general direction of petrified boy.

"Urm, yes that's right sir."

The man coughed and stood, walking from the seat and letting another, even older man take his place of judgment. "Order!"

By now, poor Clarence was feeling rather irritated by the whole situation and was wondering when he would get his opportunity to speak up for himself. "May I?" He attempted.

"You may." Said a pained looking gentleman from behind his table. He seemed a little younger than the others, but even he looked to be in his late 70's at least thought Clarence.

"Please, I would like to be allowed to return to my life. I have so much to do and feel I would have wasted the things already done."

The man stroked his chin and frowned, "Do you not think that the many other souls who attend our court wish to return to their lives?"

"Ye…" But Clarence was cut short by the judge.

"We have seen many souls here. Many men and woman who wish to be allowed access back to their lives. But this, I am afraid is not your destiny."

Clarence felt his heart drop, well he would have if he'd had a beating heart at that moment, but he felt the sadness and pain in his soul. The feeling of despair that he had felt all of his life still ran through him like a monster, picking at his mind and feelings, making him feel like he had done for as long as he could remember. "But…" He contemplated his words and his future and he realised the futility of arguing with these old men. They didn't care for his begging or for his pleas, they just kept rotating and changing and making the whole judgment more hideous than the last one, and then he finally gave in, "It's fine. I'll just die then. And be on my way."

Another man had taken the place of the other now, but this one looked even younger, perhaps in his late 50's, with his eyes brighter and his mind less jaded by an eternity of negative judgments and bitterness than the others. Clarence saw his chance now, "Please, I wish to be back with my beloved."

The judge nodded slowly as if contemplating the lads future, "So tell me. Why is your case so different from the others I have seen? Tell me why I should grant you life over those who have been returned to the place that beckons them? Why is it that YOU, Clarence Bunn should be blessed with the gift of return when the soldier who died for you must not return? Why the sailor who lost his life to the cruel sea was not allowed to see again his wife and children? Tell me Clarence Bunn… tell US, the adjudicators, why we should pity your soul in particular?"

Clarence stared at the man, at the gavel in his hand, at the mumbling, moaning, leering jeering men about him. He looked to the floor, and at his feet and he thought about his beloved Kelly. "Because I, Clarence Bunn, have never felt the warm embrace of a mother, nor have I ever had a doting father. I have not had the blessing of childhood." He looked around at the old men, "This I will never feel. It is lost now and I can never have it returned to me, not in this life time, but, I had not ever before, felt the wind in my hair nor the touch of a woman or even the feeling of friendship. Not until these past weeks. Where I have found all of these things and brought happiness to some lost souls. I have brought love to the loveless. I have brought escape to the imprisoned and I have, myself found something worth fighting for. A woman whom I have travelled half the earth to find and take back, for whom I would gladly give up my life for."

"But you did give up your life for this woman did you not? You made the sacrifice of your own soul for love as a million others have and will continue to do for the rest of time and beyond."

Clarence slowly shook his head, "I did not give up my life for her. Not willingly. I gave up my life to take a cancer from this earth. I dug into it and expelled it like a pustule. But it was not for her. It was for everyone and anyone who might be tainted by him and his touch, his words, his sickness…" He breathed out, not knowing if he had breathed at all during his rant of defence, but he knew he had tried his best and that, was the best he had.

"You have made this difficult for us Clarence Bunn and you leave us no choice…" The room seemed to erupt with a rumble and kerfuffle of words and jeers and gasps. Whispers filled the high up galleries where dusty old men shook their heads and eyed the boy with suspicion and curse.

Another man took the stand now, but he was pushed to the table in a bath chair and held an ear trumpet shakily against his head. He slumbered in his chair, a chequered rug across his knees and, with a breath so shallow it made him seem barely alive, the most ancient of men spoke, "And so... The wheels of justice... Have stopped and... Judgment must... Must... Must be passed... And so...This day... This day we must call... Upon us... The great Arbitrator." A gasp filled the hall of gentlemen and whispers hissed about he place, echoing like a hundred snakes. The great and very old man raised a hand, "Call the Arbitrator."

The rumble of benches this time filled the room as the room stood, waiting for something to happen. Clarence found himself turning as from behind came the sound of a grand door opening. "Oh my." He managed to whisper, as a black cloaked man entered the hall, his head bowed and concealed by a hood like a monk. The figure brushed past Clarence and stood at the desk, and that's when he realised who it was, "Death?" He whispered as the man lowered his hood, revealing his identity.

"Clarence Bunn." His voice was deep and rumbled through the now silent halls like an earth quake. "You are here to plead for your life back. You wish to stop your soul from entering its final stage?"

Clarence merely nodded at the man and then slowly whispered in a squeaked voice, "Yes sir."

Death, or the Arbitrator as he was know to the court, paced, arms invisibly tucked beneath his cloak, "I have heard your plea and I have read you case. I have seen for myself the things you has done, your pitiful childhood and then your transformation into a man. Why, if I had not known, I could mistake you as two people. A drastic life change." He looked around at the ancient Adjudicators, "You may not feel this young soul should be returned but I, the Arbitrator, believe he should be let go."

There was a collective gasping and hustle and bustle that went around the hall like an audible Mexican wave of disbelief. The fat judge had now returned and stood, red faced, "This is absurd. A soul cannot return for such a petty reason and for such small victories. It can not be allowed."

"But I have the final say. This boy deserved to be judged as any other, but he did not deserve the unfair treatment that he received and so, therefore, he shall be returned."

The round judge banged the gavel upon the desk, "ORDER." He shouted as the court erupted.

Death walked towards Clarence and looked down at him, still not smiling and still with his mournfully bad tempered expression, "Come along Bunn, before they get you and drag your soul to somewhere a soul aught not be dragged too."

"Can they do that?"

Death exhaled into a sigh, "Yes Bunn, they can do whatever they bloody well want, now come along and for goodness sake, don't turn round."

But Clarence happened to glance back as he followed the tall, dark and dead figure, just in time to see them starting to stand and move, but this time they moved faster and fluidly like ghosts. Their black robes now floating behind them and their legs nonexistent as they began to rise up into the air and float in a spiral around the ceiling like a black tornado, faster and faster they moved, their faces distorted now with anger and fangs. "Oh golly." Said Clarence.

"I told you not to bloody look." Growled death as he pulled the boy to walk faster.

The blackness happened again and it filled the lads eyes with that same darkness that was darker than anything the brain could comprehend. He felt his soul and body floating together, in a kind of duality, through a vacuum and then, like the waking eye, a grey light began to creep through. But this time there was no beach, there was no reverse sea and there was certainly, and rather unfortunately, no Kelly, there was just a grey, barren landscape that stretched out in every direction for an eternity. There was nothing else, and it seemed no one else until the voice startled Clarence to turn round.

"Well. You do not have much time. The wheels are turning and your life is soon to be yours again."

"Thank you so much, but I didn't know you were to be the Arbitrator." He grinned, "And you knew all along… Right?"

A raised eyebrow said a thousand words, "No Clarence. I did not know they would call for me but it would seem some spirit in some distant place was turning fate in your favour."

"You mean you didn't have anything to do with turning up? I could have just lost and been sent to… Wherever?"

"Yes."

"Wowzers, fancy that?" Clarence was genuinely shocked, "Having two such important jobs, it must be awfully tiring for you."

Death shook his head, "You seem to forget just who I am Clarence Bunn. I am Death and I see

all…" And for a moment he looked almost human as an emotion crossed his stony face, "…Besides, I have to pay the bills."
 "What?"
 "My little joke, I have no bills, I'm eternal."
 "Oh," giggled Clarence nervously. But now the grey sky began to blur and Clarence' brain began to throw a million questions up like a tombola. "Please. Before I go, how did you know so much about me? How do you see all?"
 The landscape behind Death began to drift into nothing now as the blackness replaced the limbo world like ink being poured over the grey non reality, but he heard the voice.
 "You have always been destined to be the saviour of my precious daughter and so, since your birth, you have been followed by a veil of death. Everything from your mother dying during child birth to this very moment, Death has been as much a part of your life as living."
 Clarence now felt himself drifting into the dark void again but he still called out, "What do mean? A veil of death?"
 The voice of Death was now like a thought in the boys head rather than that of a physical thing, "Look at your life Clarence. Your job. Your friends. Your one true love… Is it not strange to you that death follows you

everywhere… Look back… Look back."

"Don't look back!" The voice was now loud and American and came from above the lad. He blinked and saw the hands of his friends reaching down to him.

"Don't look down. We've got ya Clarence," shouted the Clown.

Clarence climbed a little further before the hands grabbed him, Clown and Harry taking one arm as Ace pulled the other. "My friends." He called as he reached the safety of the top, "And Clown. You remembered my name, you got it right."

Clown shrugged, "I don't get ya Craig but it's good to have ya back."

Clarence looked around at the unconscious necromancers and at the vampire and the werewolf and he shut his eyes and felt the warmth as his three companions all held him tightly, hugging him so hard that he could hardly breath. The feeling that he had craved for 19 years. The feeling of belonging and love and true friendship, but then he opened his eyes and stared forward. "But where is Kelly?"

"Clarence!"

He turned and saw the most perfect sight his eyes had ever seen. A vision that he would carry to the grave, the sight of his beloved, standing there like an angel. Her skin was pink and soft, no more was she corpse-like in a waxy exterior. Her eyes were no longer glazed and lifeless but fresh and twinkling with tears of joy.

"I thought you were gone, that you had gone back. I thought I had lost you." He held her and squeezed her tightly to him. He could feel her body against his and he could feel the life within her, he could almost feel her heart beating if he concentrated.

"No Clarence. I could not go back because I am alive and my heart beats."

"He let you stay?"

"Well he could hardly have me back after all the trouble I caused him when I was dead."

"Speaking of being dead. He told me that my life had a veil of death. What did he mean?"

"Well take a look at your life. Read back through your life's voyage and see. You had and still have a purpose here my love." There was a knowing look in the girls eyes as she stared up at him.

"What do you know dead girl?" "

"Let's just say, I think your life has only just begun Clarence Bunn."

THE END

Printed in Great Britain
by Amazon